MOLLY ON THE OUTLAW TRAIL

Molly Owens is an ace undercover detective on the trail of Cole Estes who had emptied bank vaults and robbed trains from northern Montana to New Mexico, a man who is hard to outshoot and outsmart.

The treacherous mountain passes and forbidden canyon hideouts of the Outlaw Trail are no place for a lady, but the Outlaw Trail has never seen a lady like Molly.

MOLLY ON THE OUTLAW TRAIL

Stephen Overholser

*This Book Donated
by the
Friends of the
Prescott Valley
Public Library*

GUNSMOKE

This hardback edition 2004
by BBC Audiobooks Ltd
by arrangement with
Golden West Literary Agency

ISBN 1 4056 8006 7

British Library Cataloguing in Publication Data available.

Printed and bound in Great Britain by
Antony Rowe Ltd., Chippenham, Wiltshire

MOLLY ON THE OUTLAW TRAIL

CHAPTER I

Hoofprints of a shod horse, marked by crushed blades of grass, led across the mountain meadow toward a thicket. Molly studied the fugitive's trail and was caught by surprise when her walking horse suddenly squealed and reared, violently pawing the air.

Molly landed on her backside in the spongy turf, amazed. That even-tempered buckskin gelding had never reared up before, much less thrown her.

Raising up on her elbows, she glimpsed the horse galloping away, reins and mane and tail flying. Then she heard a low grunting sound and knew why the gelding had panicked.

A dozen yards away, the grizzly bear rose up on his hind legs behind a thicket of subalpine mountain ash. Straightening to his full height of nearly six feet, the bear slowly turned his head back and forth, sniffing the air while listening with small twitching ears.

Molly shrank back, staring at that great shaggy head, her mind dizzy with fear. None of her training in self-defense techniques, the form of hand-to-hand combat based on the Japanese art of jujitsu that she'd mastered, would help her against this foe. Grizzlies were the most feared animal on the continent, and for good reason. Powerful and fast, they were enormous creatures with no natural enemies.

Molly quickly realized that the only firearm available to her, the derringer strapped in a holster on her right leg, would do nothing but anger this bear. Her Winchester rifle and Colt .38 had departed with her horse.

She'd seen grizzlies before, from a safe distance, with the benefit of field glasses, and knew this one to be a male, not quite fully grown. Bright sunlight of midday shone on his thick coat, a gold-and-brown color that was almost white at the shoulders—grizzled. The animal's vision was poor, but his senses of smell and hearing were keen, and now he was searching for an intruder.

Molly stared as the bear turned, showing the hump of muscles above his shoulders, muscles that drove his legs faster than any human could run. She remained still, fighting her own fear that commanded her to flee, and hoped the bear would not catch her scent. In time he might wander away. But then she saw blood on the claws curving out of his front paws.

Heart pounding in her chest, Molly realized the young bear was feeding and would be protective of his kill. Now he methodically sampled the air, turning his head in every direction. He dropped to all fours and came crashing out of the thicket. Molly's mouth went dry as the grizzly walked straight to her.

Neck outstretched, the big animal stopped half a dozen feet away and sniffed. Molly stared into his small brown eyes. The bear moved closer. She lay down, hoping to appear passive and unthreatening.

She heard the bear sniffing in quick gusts of air, and after several moments saw him turn away and amble back toward the thicket. A vast sense of relief swept over Molly, and she drew a deep breath. But just as the grizzly reached the thicket, he whirled with a quickness that was terrifying and charged her.

Molly sat up and involuntarily screamed. The bear plowed to a halt a few feet away and cocked his head. He eased forward slowly, sniffing again. Molly's nostrils filled with his strong odor when the grizzly reached her, nearly touching her face with his dark, wet nose.

Barely in control of her surging fear, Molly sat still as the bear examined her. The grizzly was clearly annoyed by her presence, yet undecided about what to do. An adult grizzly probably would have slain her by now.

Feeling the bear's hot breath on her face, Molly spoke softly. The bear backed away. Molly swallowed and spoke again in what she hoped was a soothing voice. The grizzly sat down in the grass and cocked his head, listening.

"I won't hurt you . . . I won't take your food . . ."

The bear yawned, showing his large tongue, red mouth, and yellowed teeth. Mouth closed, he blinked slowly and raised up on all fours. He came toward Molly again. This time he circled her, baring his teeth and growling. After making a complete circle, he lunged forward, biting her leg above the boot top.

Molly screamed. She jumped to her feet. Shrieking, she waved her arms. The bear backed away, and Molly turned and ran.

The grizzly thundered across the meadow after her, quickly closing the distance. Molly heard him coming, heard his paws pounding the earth, heard his sharp breaths and growls, and then she felt his teeth sink into her calf.

She fell, and the bear was on top of her.

Rolling on her back, Molly struggled to escape. The grizzly pinned her to the ground with one paw and swatted her head with the other. The pad of his paw struck above her temple, his claws raking her Stetson. Growling now, he opened his great mouth and came for her throat.

Molly's ears rang from the blow, and her mind swam crazily. She could not believe she was about to die a painful death, but as she reached out to grasp the bear's shaggy neck, she knew this was not a dream, knew she was powerless to stop him.

She grabbed thick fur at the grizzly's neck. Holding her arms stiff at the elbows, she tried to push him away. She could not, but as the bared teeth came down, she slid away a few inches.

Frustrated, the bear growled and gave a violent shake of his head, breaking her grasp. He came for her throat again, saliva dripping from his open mouth, and this time Molly knew she could not stop him.

The loud clattering sound that erupted and suddenly filled her ears was strange and unrecognizable, a weird metallic sound that was loud and offensive. Now Molly thought she really was living a nightmare, a violent dream at once real and bizarre.

The grizzly leaped away. He rose to his hind legs. The clattering sound continued, and grew louder. The bear turned his head toward it and dropped to all fours. Turning, he ambled off in the opposite direction.

Molly rolled on her side, looking through her tears toward the loud noise. In the meadow forty yards away stood a boy. Dressed in faded overalls, a flannel shirt, and a floppy-brimmed felt hat, he held a coffee can in his hands. He shook the can vigorously until the grizzly loped into the trees at the far edge of the meadow.

Molly was not the fainting type, but as she watched the boy run across the meadow toward her, hat flying off his head to expose red hair, she nearly passed out. She was filled with both gratitude and disbelief that he had frightened the grizzly away.

"Lady, lady!" he cried. "You hurt? How bad are you hurt?"

Running at full speed, he skidded to his knees at Molly's side. He breathlessly repeated, "How bad are you hurt, lady?"

Molly sat up, not finding her voice for a moment. "Thank you . . . thank you for . . . scaring that bear. . . . How did you . . . ?"

The boy held up the Arbuckle coffee can and gave it a shake. "Stones inside. The noise frightens bears, hurts their ears, I guess. Grandpa Barney won't let me leave the cabin without it."

Still dazed, Molly stared at this thin, green-eyed boy until she became aware of a throbbing pain in her left leg below her knee. Bending forward, she pulled up that side of her riding skirt. Blood oozed from two sets of punctures high on her calf where she'd been bitten.

"Goddamn," the boy whispered.

Gingerly wiping blood away, Molly was relieved to see that her flesh was not torn. Blood seeped from the wounds, but was not flowing. No large blood vessels had been severed.

"I'm all right," Molly said, pulling her divided skirt down to her boot tops, "or I will be as soon as I get a bandage around my leg." She got to her feet, favoring her left leg. "First, I have to find my horse."

"I caught him," the boy said, jumping to his feet. He was nearly as tall as Molly, and she guessed his age to be thirteen or fourteen. "He was running hell for leather through the trees," the boy went on, "but I caught him. Big buckskin gelding, isn't he?"

Molly nodded.

He pointed over his shoulder to a stand of blue-spruce trees. "I tied him over yonder. I heard you scream, and that's why I came running."

Molly thanked him again and held out her hand. "I'm Molly Owens."

"Buck's my name," the boy said with a grin. "Glad I could help you out of a fix." He added, "You know, I found a horse yesterday, too, running wild like yours, saddled and everything." He possessed an intense manner and spoke in barrages of staccato words.

"What kind of horse?" Molly asked.

"A mare," he replied. "Little black mare with a white blaze across her face."

Molly turned. She looked at the growth of mountain ash, trying to see through the leafy branches. "You'd better wait here."

"How come?" Buck asked.

Molly did not answer, but walked slowly toward the thicket, aware that the boy followed. Her heart raced. Even though she'd seen the bear leave, she still needed all her strength to walk to that thicket.

Edging around it, Molly saw the gnawed remains

of a human hand. Behind her, Buck suddenly swore and backed away.

The corpse was mutilated, but recognizable. His name was Hiram Galt. He'd embezzled $7,834.42 from the Colorado Bank & Trust in Denver, and Molly's investigation following the bank audit had sent the man into flight. He was a bank clerk, not a horseman or outdoorsman, and Molly had had little trouble reading his day-old trail. But until Buck had described the mare, she had not expected the trail to end here, this way.

She bent down over the corpse and removed a blood-caked money belt, then straightened up and limped away. Buck stood still, his angular face pale. When Molly reached him, she put an arm around his shoulders, and they walked out of the meadow together.

CHAPTER II

Molly and Buck rode double on the big gelding, traveling up the slope of a high ridge overlooking the meadow and then dropping down into a lush valley on the other side.

Surrounded by forests of pines and blue-spruce trees, the valley was almost hidden, a world apart, with peaceful sounds of birds and squirrels and a gentle breeze whispering through the treetops. Molly looked down through a break in the trees and saw a sky-reflecting creek meandering through high grass. The field of grass was sprinkled with colorful wildflowers.

Buck had recovered from the shock of seeing a corpse and talked steadily as the horse moved down through the trees toward the valley floor. He told rambling stories of dangers he'd faced in these mountains, yarns that featured him as the hero. They sounded farfetched, and Molly would have disbelieved every word if she had not just experienced a real adventure in which her life had been spared by this lanky red-headed boy.

The horse broke out of the trees at the bottom. Molly guided him through the grass toward a log cabin nestled at the tree line across the valley. The cabin was windowless, and the thick logs were weathered to a pale gray color. The shake roof sagged in the middle like a swaybacked nag.

After splashing across the creek, Molly saw a lean-to beside the cabin where two animals watched them approach. One was a long-eared mule; the other was a coal-black horse with a white blaze across its face.

"I do all the work around here," Buck said extravagantly. He pointed to a stump with a double-bitted ax sticking out of it. "I cut our firewood and kindling, and I build a fire every morning."

As Molly reined up, Buck pointed to the gurgling stream thirty yards away. "I wash all of our clothes over there, and most days I catch trout out of the creek for supper." He added in a lower voice, "Grandpa Barney can't do much for himself, so he depends on me."

Molly heard a note of pride in the boy's voice. He jumped off the back of the gelding and ran into the cabin, leaving the door standing open behind him.

"Grandpa, someone's here—a lady's here!"

Molly felt a stab of pain as she swung down from the saddle and put weight on her injured leg. She limped toward the cabin door. Buck appeared there.

"Grandpa wants to meet you," he said excitedly. "Come in."

Molly ducked through the low doorway and entered the cabin. The floor was dirt. As her eyes adjusted to the dim light, she saw few furnishings: a chair and a stool around a small table fashioned from warped boards, and along the wall to her right stood a sheet-iron stove.

"This is Miss Molly Owens, Grandpa," Buck announced.

"Thought I broke you of calling me 'Grandpa,'" came a growling voice from the shadows on the other side of the cabin.

Molly turned. Peering through the gloom, she made out a hunched figure rising up from a bunk. He moved toward her, walking in a rocking, uneven gait.

"Howdy, ma'am," he said, holding out a gnarled hand. "Name's Barney. Barney . . . Johnson." He spoke the last name in a way that suggested he had either not used it in a long time or had invented it.

Molly felt as though she'd grasped a handful of

loosely connected bones when she shook the old-timer's hand. Now that he stood in the light from the doorway, she saw that he was toothless, bent, and seemed to scowl. Thin strands of white hair fell down around his ears.

Molly recognized the breed. Barney was a hermit, driven into these mountains by the pressures of society, a crime committed, or a mysterious compulsion to be alone. Two generations ago he might have turned out differently. He might have been a trapper or an explorer in the West, a loner who would later be revered in school history books.

"The boy tells me you got chewed by a grizzly," Barney said. "Any truth to it?"

"I'm not lying!" Buck exclaimed.

"He saved my life," Molly said, and briefly described her encounter with the bear.

Barney grunted and gave Molly a once-over. "Well, this ain't no time fer a lady's modesty. Sit down, and throw your leg up so's I can have a look." He half-turned and pulled the chair out from the table.

"I'm not hurt too badly," Molly said. She sat down and drew up the left side of her riding skirt to her thigh. For a long moment, both the old man and the boy stared longingly at her shapely leg.

Molly smiled. She was a full-breasted woman, slender at the waist, with a sweeping curve of hips filling out her riding skirt. She was not unaccustomed to the attentions of men.

"What do you think?" she asked, lifting her leg.

Barney cleared his throat and stirred into action. He found a length of cloth near his bunk and ordered Buck to draw a pan of hot water from the stove. Dipping the cloth into the steaming water, he expertly washed her wounds, then bandaged her leg with a strip of heavy cotton.

Watching the old-timer work, Molly saw that he was not as frail as he first appeared. His clawlike hands were steady. Molly realized he was better able to take care of himself than Buck had led her to believe.

"The boy blabbered something about a dead man over the ridge," Barney said, straightening up. "That true, ma'am?"

"Damn right, it's true," Buck said defensively.

Barney snapped, "No cussing in the lady's company."

Molly suppressed a smile. "It's true."

"Well, if you wasn't riding with him," Barney asked, "how'd you come to be there by yourself?"

"I was following him," Molly said. "I've been on his trail for three days. The man was a fugitive."

Barney drew back. "You the law?"

"No," Molly said. Reaching into her handbag, she brought out a brass badge. "I'm an operative for the Fenton Investigative Agency."

"An investigator," Buck said in amazement. "I'll be good goddamned."

"Boy, get outside!" Barney said. "Go tend the lady's horse."

Buck bowed his head, then slowly obeyed.

Barney studied Molly for several moments after the boy was gone. "I reckon I shouldn't be surprised. In the Civil War some of the best spies we had was women." He paused, seeming to search for words. "I'm damned if I know what I'm going to do about that boy."

"He's not your grandson, is he?" Molly asked.

Barney shook his head. "I ain't got no kin." He rubbed his gnarled hands together, then said, "He showed up about a month ago, half-starved. I took him in and fed him. At first, he wouldn't say a word. But then he got to talking and ain't hardly stopped since. Wears me out, I'll tell you. Tells the wildest yarns, believe you me."

"Where is his family?" Molly asked.

"That's what I'm getting at," Barney said, as though she should have realized he was making a point. "See, he was telling me all these damned lies, so I finally told him to quit. 'Quit lying,' I says, 'or I'll throw you out and bolt the damned door behind you.' "

Barney paused. "Damned if he didn't start bawling. You'da thought I buried a knife in his back."

"The truth must have been painful," Molly said.

Barney nodded. "When he got through with his bawling, he told me he never knew his mother, and he got passed around from one family to another, from relatives to preachers and so on, and finally wound up in some place called the Payton Home, something like that."

"It's in Denver," Molly said. The Mike Payton Home for Boys was an orphanage, built and financed by a wealthy gold miner, himself an orphan.

"Well, the boy ran off from there," Barney said, "something he made a habit of, the way I get it, only this time he was going to hike to Wyoming to hunt fer his pa."

"Buck knows who his father is?" Molly asked.

"Sure he does," Barney said. He paused. "I'd bet a gold poke you've heard of him—Cole Estes."

Molly raised her eyebrows in surprise. Cole Estes was the leader of an outlaw gang that had gained notoriety and a certain amount of popularity by staging large holdups but never robbing individuals. The gang held up large banks, usually owned by Eastern investors, and they preyed on trains passing through remote stretches of Wyoming and Montana. Cole Estes himself was known to be a well-dressed and well-spoken man. Between jobs, he lived respectably under false names.

"Buck's telling the truth about Cole?" Molly asked.

"Fer once, I think he is," Barney said. "The hurt on that boy's face writ the truth."

CHAPTER III

In the afternoon the three of them rode back to the meadow and retrieved the body of Hiram Galt. The young grizzly was nowhere to be seen, but as a precaution, Barney stood guard with an ancient buffalo rifle while Molly wrapped the mutilated body in a blanket.

Buck kept his distance, but when Molly needed help in lifting the corpse, he clenched his jaw and did it. Together they draped the body over the back of the mare. Molly secured it with a length of rope.

The sun was sinking behind a jagged peak on the western horizon by the time they reached the cabin. Molly and Barney rode their mounts, and Buck came along behind on foot, leading the black mare.

After the animals were cared for, Molly sat in the grass in front of the cabin, her bandaged leg propped up on a length of stove wood. Buck came out of the cabin carrying a willow branch. A line was tied to it, and on the end was a fishhook.

Molly watched while the boy overturned rocks near the creek bank. He gathered up a handful of earthworms and dropped them into his shirt pocket. With great concentration he threaded one of the squirming worms onto the barbed hook.

Molly saw Buck move with a boy's craftiness toward the creek, kneeling into the grass when he drew near a deep pool. He tossed the line into quiet water below a small boulder.

Seconds later, the willow doubled over. Buck let

out a whoop and leaned back. After a brief tug of war, he pulled a trout out of the water.

The glimmering trout, more than a foot long, flopped madly in the grass. Buck scrambled after it. When he caught it, he held the struggling fish up for Molly to see, then promptly killed it by dashing its head against a stone.

In the next quarter of an hour Buck caught three more trout of the same size, all within a thirty-yard stretch of the creek. Molly watched while he knelt at water's edge and gutted the fish with his pocketknife. When he finished, he came striding back toward the cabin, grinning.

After an evening meal of trout rolled in cornmeal and fried in bacon grease, hot corn cakes topped with honey, and then peach halves from a can, Molly helped Buck wash the tin plates and flatware. Barney stretched out on his bunk.

The work done, Molly limped outside. Night had fallen, and stars shone brightly in the night sky. She sat in the grass and leaned back against the logs of the cabin, breathing deeply. The crisp air was pine-scented.

This high country of the Rockies was her favorite. The air was fine, the water cold and clear as diamonds. The colors of the blooming wildflowers were intense reds, yellows, blues, and flaming oranges, and the green grass in the valley reached to her boot tops. "Pure" was the word that came to her mind when she thought of the high country. Every plant and every creature seemed pure and clean here—even the grizzly.

Mosquitoes sang in her ears. Molly waved them away as Buck came out of the cabin and sat down in the grass beside her. A match flared, and she turned to see him touch the flame to a battered pipe in his mouth. He puffed and exhaled a great cloud of smoke.

"Best way to keep the skeeters from eating you alive," he said casually.

"I'll remember that," Molly said.

Puffing extravagantly, Buck went on to explain that he had learned from Barney to stretch precious tobacco by mixing in used coffee grounds.

He smoked awhile longer, then took the pipe out of his mouth and said, "If you have some idea of taking me back to that goddamned orphanage, you can forget it."

Molly looked at him, realizing he'd overhead her conversation with Barney. The boy's face was silhouetted against pale lamplight coming out of the cabin doorway. Buck was at an age that held him poised between boyhood and manhood, and at times he drifted into one or the other. While fishing, he'd been all boy, filled with spontaneous delight and pride. Now he was in another mood, one that brought him closer to manhood.

"You're old enough to make that decision for yourself," Molly said. She added, "I don't know how old you are, but you act like you're sixteen or seventeen."

Buck paused, obviously measuring his alternatives for an answer. "I'm fourteen," he said at last.

Molly was glad he'd told what she believed to be the truth. She wanted to build a bond of truthfulness between them. "That was not easy today, bringing the body back."

"I didn't know if I could do it," he said.

"Well, you did," Molly said. She added, "But I understand you're facing a much bigger problem."

"What do you mean?" he asked.

"You want to locate your father in Wyoming," Molly said, "but you're up here in the Colorado Rockies on foot."

"I'll get me a saddle horse one day," Buck said. "I almost owned that black mare."

"It's a stolen horse," Molly said. "You don't need that kind of problem." She paused. "Experienced lawmen and bounty hunters have tried to bring in Cole Estes. None of them have done the job."

"My father's too smart for them," Buck said. "But I'm not a lawman. I'm his son. I'll find him."

"What's your plan?" Molly asked.

Buck did not reply immediately. "I've read every newspaper article about my father that was ever written. He rides the Outlaw Trail. I figure I can get a lead on him in the Hole-in-the-Wall up in Wyoming or Robbers Roost out in Utah."

As the boy spoke, Molly began to suspect that he might not be trying so hard to find his father. He had an idea, but no real plan. Perhaps the threat of rejection from his father loomed large in his private thoughts.

"Buck," Molly said, "I can never repay you for saving my life. But I might be able to do something else for you."

"What?" he asked, puffing on the pipe.

"Find your father," she said.

"You can?" he asked, jerking the pipe out of his mouth.

"I can try," Molly said. "But I think you should come back to Denver with me."

"Oh, no," Buck said. "I told you I'm not going back to that place—"

"You don't have to," Molly said. "I have something else in mind."

CHAPTER IV

"I declare, Molly, I can understand how you feel about that boy, but he's full of the devil, full up to the ears. That's where he gets his red hair, if you ask me."

Molly smiled as she reclined against the back of the settee in the solarium of Mrs. Boatwright's Boardinghouse for Ladies. Mrs. Boatwright had just explained how Buck had cleverly relieved the iceman of half a dozen extra blocks of ice during yesterday's delivery.

"I'll speak to him," Molly said, shifting her bandaged leg on the leather ottoman in front of the settee. "With a little prodding, he'll live up to our agreement."

"I hope so, Molly, I surely do," Mrs. Boatwright said. "And you'll have to speak to him again about his cursing, too."

The angular features of the landlady's face clearly showed her annoyance. But she was not a woman easily angered, and she had agreed without hesitation to Molly's plan for letting Buck live here in exchange for his work.

"Your leg still painful?" she asked.

Molly shrugged. "It's healing."

"My goodness, but you're lucky to be alive," Mrs. Boatwright said. "Ever since you got back, I've had nightmares about being eaten by a bear. You really shouldn't travel alone as you do."

"I prefer it," Molly said, smiling at the woman's concern. She knew Mrs. Boatwright had come to regard her almost as a daughter, and with a mother's

16

concern she barely concealed her disapproval of Molly's chosen profession and the dangers that came with it.

Molly admired this sturdy woman. Half a dozen years ago, upon the sudden death of her husband, Mrs. Boatwright emerged from her grief to find herself heir to an enormous debt. Her husband's success, explained the family banker, had been a facade for the last several years. Mining ventures had regularly failed, and when the bottom went out of the silver market, he was just about finished. The estate consisted only of the brick-and-marble mansion built in happier times in Denver's elite Capitol Hill district. Creditors now clamored for the place.

In her fifties at the time, Mrs. Boatwright not only had been shielded from her husband's declining finances but also knew practically nothing about business or industry. She possessed a strong will, however, and a determination to make the symbol of her husband's failure into a success. After convincing the family banker to advance her enough cash to satisfy the most urgent demands of her late husband's creditors, she turned her lavish home into a boardinghouse for ladies of means.

"I just sat myself down after the funeral," Mrs. Boatwright once told Molly, "and I thought, *Now, what do I know how to do?* Well, the answer came to me: I know how to run a household. I know how to manage hired help, from French chefs to Irish maids, and I know people. So that's how I decided to start the most elegant boardinghouse west of the Mississippi."

Success did not come quickly, but after the third year of operation, when Molly moved in, Mrs. Boatwright had proved herself. The creditors had been paid off, and her regular payments to the bank had put a smile on the thin face of the family banker.

Mrs. Boatwright took a personal interest in all the women who boarded with her, partly—as she once confessed to Molly—out of her desire for family and partly because she had learned the widsom of spotting well-dressed deadbeats as quickly as possible.

All of her ten boarders were wealthy women, of ages ranging from middle twenties to middle seventies, and all shared a desire for the highest quality in food and furnishings. The youngest resident was a homely, rather desperate girl from Boston who wore silk dresses from Paris and attended all the balls and social events of the year. The oldest was Esther Raines, a demanding, shrill-voiced crone who always— even at breakfast—wore long black dresses and much diamond jewelry.

Molly smiled to herself and thought: Now, add to them one rowdy fourteen-year-old boy, and life around Mrs. Boatwright's boardinghouse was bound never to be quite the same again.

Later in the afternoon, after a long, refreshing nap, Molly dressed and went downstairs, following a back hallway that led to the mansion's rear entrance and the basement staircase.

Molly descended the stairs. Beside the massive coal furnace was a furnished room, once occupied by Mr. Boatwright's attendant. Now Buck lived there.

Molly knocked on the door, and after several moments Buck opened it. Still dressed in the new clothes he wore to his lessons with his tutor, Buck did not look much different from other boys in Denver. His red hair was cropped short, and he was scrubbed clean.

"What's new in the Roman Empire?" Molly asked.

"Cicero was beheaded," Buck said. He grinned and raised his arm, bringing it down swiftly in a chopping motion. "His head went rolling through the sand, the way the professor told it."

"Politics," Molly said.

Buck shrugged. "I don't see the point in reading that stuff. It all happened a long time ago, a lot of miles from here."

"Wasn't it Cicero who said that not to know what happened before we were born is to remain a child?" Molly asked.

Buck nodded as he considered that idea. "I guess that's why I want to find my father. I'll find out what happened a long time ago, and I won't remain a child."

"I'll keep my end of our agreement," Molly said, "when I start my investigation tomorrow."

Buck grew excited. "You sure you won't need my help?"

"I work alone," Molly said, "but if the time comes when I need help, I'll tell you." She paused. "Mrs. Boatwright tells me that you helped the iceman with his delivery yesterday."

Buck looked downward but said nothing.

"Better let the deliverymen do their own work from now on," Molly said.

"All right," Buck said, glancing at her.

"I know it isn't easy living here," Molly said.

"That's the whole damned truth," Buck said. "Old Lady Boatwright watches every move I make. Yesterday she threw out my pipe. Said it stunk. Then she got after me for cussing." He looked at Molly in frustration. "Hell, I wasn't even cussing her."

"This is her home," Molly said, "and I did warn you that you'd have to live by her rules. And you'll have to admit it's better than the orphanage."

Buck nodded slowly. "Don't worry, I'll do what you said. And I'll do the chores around here—until you find my father."

Molly looked at him, hoping she had not promised too much. She had told Buck that she might not be able to locate Cole Estes, and that if she did, the outlaw might not even admit Buck's existence. Still, Molly realized, Buck had high hopes.

In the morning the telegraphed message Molly had been expecting was delivered to the mansion. She took it into the sunny solarium, sat in a wicker rocker, and opened the envelope.

Operative Molly Owens:

I am grieved to learn of your injuries, and hope your recovery is progressing smoothly. Please keep me informed. Should you incur medical expenses, notify me for reimbursement. And by all means, take the vacation you request, as much time as you require for complete recovery. We should all be grateful that you were not injured more seriously.

Despite the tragic and terrifying end you described in your report of the investigation, your work was most successful. I offer my congratulations for a job well done. The president of the Colorado Bank & Trust is satisfied that an important precedent has been established in his institution, and he is confident that in the future, embezzlers will apply for positions in banks other than his.

My sincere thanks for conducting the investigation and bringing it to a successful conclusion. I hope the coming days will be restful ones for you out there in the "wild" West.

> Horace J. Fenton, President
> Fenton Investigation Agency
> New York City, N.Y.

The first question to be answered took Molly to the Mike Payton Home for Boys.

In the headmaster's office of the brick-and-granite building Molly learned that Oliver James Estes had been a troublesome resident here. A frequent runaway, he returned with a mouthful of improbable stories and inevitably engaged other boys in fistfights when they doubted his tales of adventure. He was taunted by boys who called him "Red" and who chanted, "Red, Red, wet the bed." For this reason, the headmaster told Molly, the boy insisted on being called "Buck," a name he'd evidently borrowed from a cowboy he had met during a time when he had run away from the Payton Home.

Molly sensed that the headmaster was more relieved than concerned when Buck had departed this last time, and now quickly agreed with her that the boy would be better off for the time being in the Boatwright mansion.

And it was true, Molly learned from birth records on file at the Payton Home, that Oliver James Estes was the son of Cole Estes.

Molly next went to the United States marshal's office in downtown Denver. Her left leg ached as she climbed a staircase to the third floor. There she found a clerk in a file room and introduced herself.

The clerk came out from behind his desk, a pale, bespectacled young man wearing sleeve garters and baggy pants held up by suspenders. He took her past a bulletin board that was crowded with reward posters to a row of oak file cabinets.

"There," he said, pointing to a drawer containing published accounts and handwritten reports of the Cole Estes gang. Molly opened the drawer and saw that it was nearly full. She pulled up a chair and started reading.

Exploits of the gang ranged from northern Montana to the southern reaches of New Mexico. Bank vaults had been emptied out and express cars had been robbed in those states as well as in Utah, Wyoming, and Colorado.

Over the past decade the Cole Estes gang ranged in size from three men to six or eight. Molly scanned their names in the files, recognizing several she knew to be dead or serving prison terms: Ned Stilson, Claud Snyder, Rufus Brown, Sam Parris, Tulsa Jack Kerns, Del Vincente.

Many other outlaws were suspected of taking part in the gang's robberies over the years, but only two were named consistently: Matt Bledsoe and Pony Diehl.

Matt Bledsoe was often described in the reports as Cole Estes' "lieutenant," and was known to be very loyal and a man of some courage. Pony Diehl's reputation rested on his ability to handle firearms, particularly a rifle with a telescopic sight he was known to carry. Many a pursuing posse had been turned back by long-range, pinpoint shooting attributed to Pony Diehl.

Cole Estes himself was regarded as a brilliant tactician. Experienced lawmen who generally had low regard for outlaws credited Cole Estes with the ability to plan a robbery with the care and attention to detail of a general plotting a battle.

Wearing simple disguises, Estes would open an account in a bank, and return often enough to cause the employees to remember his charm. He was secretly looking for the bank's vulnerabilities. Escape routes were well planned, with fresh horses left in strategic places along the way.

Cole Estes was known to boast that he had never killed a man, but Molly noted that on several occasions lawmen and bystanders were wounded during and after robberies. If none of these people had died from their wounds, Estes could hardly claim credit. The truth, she suspected, was that Cole Estes never actually set out to kill anyone.

He had earned something of a Robin Hood reputation by never robbing passengers on a train his gang had stopped, and he never robbed country banks that served ranches and farms. And when he "borrowed" a horse while fleeing a posse, he sent back payment to the owner.

"Where's that new reward dodger on Cole Estes?"

Molly looked up from her reading and saw the man who had entered the room. Wearing a dirty, shapeless hat and a soiled duster that reached to his boot tops, he stood between the clerk's desk and the bulletin board.

"It's right behind you," the clerk said without looking up from his work.

"Ten thousand dollars will be paid out by Union Pacific, ain't that right?" the man asked. "Dead or alive?"

"Yes, sir, just as it says there."

When the man turned toward the bulletin board, his duster fell open and Molly saw the bone grips of a large revolver holstered on his hip. Now his body odor wafted through the room.

"I don't read good," he said.

The clerk looked up, wrinkling his nose. After a moment he left his desk and came around to the bulletin board. He read aloud:

$10,000 REWARD

WANTED

DEAD OR ALIVE

COLE ESTES

ROBBERY

$10,000 reward to be paid in cash by the Union Pacific Railroad Company for the capture dead or alive of the outlaw COLE ESTES, identified while robbing the U.P. mail coach on May 16, 1895, seven miles west of Rock Springs, Wyoming.

DESCRIPTION: medium height
reddish hair
green eyes
known to be well-dressed, quiet-mannered
known to have preference for white quarter-horse geldings

The man grunted when the clerk finished reading. Molly saw the bespectacled clerk retreat a step while casting a questioning look at the man.

"Do you know the whereabouts of Cole Estes?"

Like an alarmed animal, the man made a sudden growling sound and glared at the clerk. "If I did, I sure as hell wouldn't be telling you." He turned abruptly and strode out of the room, his spurs ringing.

The clerk looked at Molly and made a show of holding his nose. "Bounty hunter."

CHAPTER V

By lamplight that night Molly packed clothes in her valise and then cleaned and oiled her revolver and derringer. The revolver, nickel-plated with scrollwork on the frame, was a Colt double-action Lightning model .38 with a two-and-a-half-inch barrel.

The compact revolver fit in her leather handbag with the other tools of her trade—half a dozen magnifying lenses, a ring of master skeleton keys, and a set of lock probes. The revolver had the stopping power of a larger handgun, yet was small enough to be carried in a shoulder holster that fit inconspicuously under a jacket or cape. Her backup firearm, the two-shot derringer, was carried in a small holster strapped to her right leg.

In the morning Buck carried her valise out to the waiting carriage. Molly paused in the entryway while Mrs. Boatwright told her why she should not go off on another trip so soon.

"Your leg isn't healed," she said, "and you shouldn't be walking on it for at least a week."

"I'll be sitting in train coaches and Concord stages for the next three days," Molly said. "Don't worry. I'll be all right. The question is, can you handle Buck while I'm gone?"

"Oh my, yes," Mrs. Boatwright said, waving her hand to dismiss any suggestion of a problem. "We'll get along like a pair of lovebirds."

Molly smiled and gave the woman a good-bye hug. She walked outside and descended the marble staircase to the graveled drive, where Buck stood beside the carriage.

"Won't take me a minute to get my stuff," Buck said.

Molly shook her head and saw the boy's face turn red when she leaned forward and kissed his cheek. "Take good care of Mrs. Boatwright while I'm gone," she whispered.

Molly took the morning train to Cheyenne, where she changed trains and rode the Union Pacific west-bound across the high plains of southern Wyoming. The dry, hot land appeared withered, dotted with greasewood and sagebrush and stretches of short grass. From the window of the passenger coach Molly saw small herds of antelope but few other signs of life. The antelope turned their white rumps and ran from the lonely wail of the steam engine's whistle.

After midnight she awakened when the train jerked to a stop in Rock Springs. In the black night, with its silence broken by the huffing steam engine, Molly found her way to a hotel on the narrow main street leading away from the depot.

In the morning the sun was hot and brassy, and she came out of the hotel, blinking against the glare. To the north she saw flat-topped hills, capped with stone, but in other directions the vast, empty land stretched out as far as she could see.

Molly walked along the main street of Rock Springs to the town marshal's office. The frame buildings here, unpainted, had weathered to a gray-brown color that was remarkably similar to the color of the land.

Across the tracks Molly saw the remains of China-town, a scene of violence a decade ago. The Union Pacific coal mines were nearby, and during a strike, the company imported trainloads of Chinese laborers. This attempt at strikebreaking led to riots, and more than two dozen unarmed Chinese were murdered. Across the country, this carnage became known as the Rock Springs Massacre.

Molly saw the dilapidated shacks built of old boards,

packing crates, flattened tin cans, and anything the Chinese could find to build their town. Now most of them were gone. They had never mingled with the whites, and in the years after the massacre, they returned to the West Coast.

The town marshal's office and jail was one of the few brick buildings in town. Molly entered and saw the marshal slumped in the chair behind his desk, rubbing his eyes. He looked up when the door closed.

"Long night, marshal?" Molly asked, smiling. She crossed the room.

The marshal grinned and stood. He wore a handlebar mustache, and his dark hair was combed straight back from his forehead. A square-shouldered man, he had a look of physical power about him.

"Drunk railroaders fighting drunk coal miners," the marshal said. He jerked his head toward the steel-reinforced door to his right. "I won."

Molly held out her hand to shake and introduced herself.

"I'm Sam Darnell," the marshal said, grasping her hand in his firm grip. "A lady Fenton operative, huh? Who are you tracking?"

"Cole Estes," Molly said.

Marshal Darnell did not laugh aloud, but he failed to hide his smile. "Cole Estes," he repeated.

"I'd like some information about the train robbery west of here," Molly said. "Who was in on it, which direction they went after the robbery, and so on."

Darnell studied her, as though wondering whether or not to take this woman seriously. At last he motioned to the armchair beside his desk and then sat down.

"From the descriptions we got from the U.P. crew," he said, "it appears the Cole Estes gang joined forces with Billy Truax and his bunch of killers. Six men stopped the train, and Billy Truax is believed to have gunned down the conductor."

"Seems like that big reward ought to be offered for his capture," Molly said, "rather than for Cole Estes."

Darnell shook his head. "Billy Truax doesn't have brains enough to stop a train, much less blow a safe in the baggage car. No, the U.P. is determined to put Cole Estes out of action. Take the leader away from those outlaws, and you'll go a long ways toward stopping them."

"Who else took part in the robbery?" Molly asked.

"Matt Bledsoe and Pony Diehl were recognized," Darnell said. "The other two men weren't."

"Did a posse ride after them?" Molly asked.

The marshal nodded. "Trailed them south a ways, but the long arm of the law came up short." He paused. "I don't know if the posse lost the trail or turned back out of good sense."

"What do you mean?" Molly asked.

"That's rough country out there," he said. "Dry and hot. If a man doesn't know where the water holes are, he'll die under the sun. And if a lawman doesn't die of thirst, he'll likely get a case of lead poisoning in Robbers Roost."

Molly had read of the famous hideout on the Outlaw Trail. Men on the run would ride deep into the Utah desert, fleeing certain death on the gallows while gambling that they would survive the trek into the Roost. The Outlaw Trail itself led lawbreakers north and south for the entire length of the United States, from the Little Rockies of northern Montana to the Hole-in-the Wall of Wyoming, Brown's Hole in northwestern Colorado, Robbers Roost in Utah, and on south to hideouts in New Mexico. Of all of them, Robbers Roost was the most forbidding.

"Cole Estes is there?" Molly asked.

Darnell shrugged. "All I know for certain is that the posse trailed the gang to Wild Horse and into the desert a ways."

Molly asked, "What's Wild Horse—a town?"

"No, it's just a stage stop and road ranch," he replied. He studied her and added, "A place where strangers aren't questioned when they buy supplies at triple the usual prices."

"Thank you, marshal," Molly said, standing. "You've been very helpful."

Darnell quickly got to his feet. "Now, hold on, Miss Owens. Where are you headed from here—if you don't mind my asking."

"Wild Horse," she said.

"Well, now," he said, shaking his head, "I'd sure admire to talk you out of that. I know you Fenton operatives are well-trained in investigative work, but it just isn't a good idea for a stranger to make a ride out of Wild Horse, much less a woman alone trying to bust into Robbers Roost—"

"Marshal," Molly interrupted, "I genuinely appreciate your concern." She smiled at him. "But I can take care of myself."

CHAPTER VI

Molly traveled south out of Rock Springs, Wyoming, on the lonely road to Vernal, Utah, in a battered mud wagon pulled by four scrubby horses.

She had hoped to make the trip in a gently rocking Concord stagecoach, not a bouncing, clattering vehicle like this one. The mud wagon had a canvas top and side curtains that could be rolled down to keep out the dust, but closing them made the heat nearly unbearable. Molly and the other two passengers, a drummer and an elderly lady, finally agreed it was best to leave the side curtains open and cover their mouths with neckerchiefs.

"Now we look like a bunch of bandits," the lady remarked with a cackle.

Conversation was difficult in the rattling wagon, and after the first hour of travel, they fell silent, looking dully out at the barren landscape. The drummer carried a samples case on his lap. He wore a dark suit, and on his upper lip was a pencil-thin mustache. When he caught Molly's eye, he leered and winked at her. She turned in her seat and stared out at the desert.

The wagon stopped at Vernal. Molly and the other passengers spent the night in a small hotel next to the stage station. At departure, early in the morning, an enormous woman climbed aboard, settling in beside Molly. While the other two passengers dozed as the mud wagon rolled southward, the woman confided to Molly that she was traveling to Greenriver to marry a man she'd met through correspondence. He had promised to meet her at the Greenriver station with a bouquet of flowers in hand.

The land became increasingly desolate and vast. Molly watched a lone hawk circle in the pale sky, but she saw no other signs of life. Far in the distance, a heat wave shimmered where the desert met the sky.

All the passengers but Molly got off at Greenriver. While the luggage was being taken out of the boot at the rear of the wagon, Molly saw the fat woman hurry into the stage station, then come out and look around, her face lined with worry. No one claimed her. Molly wondered if one of the shaggy men lounging in the shade of the building was the correspondent, now cursed with cold feet and second thoughts.

After the team of horses was changed, the wagon pulled out. Molly sat alone in the coach, her mind dulled by heat and boredom. The journey to Wild Horse seemed endless, as though the narrow road had become a treadmill, and after a supper stop at a small road ranch where the team was changed again, Molly slept in the tossing, bouncing wagon. She came awake in full darkness, realizing the mud wagon had stopped. The driver pulled the door open.

"Wild Horse," he said, lifting a lantern.

Molly climbed down by the lantern's light, and waited at the rear wheel while the driver pulled her valise out of the boot. She saw a bearded man come out of the stage station and was aware that he regarded her with silent curiosity while the driver climbed back up to the seat. With a shout and a slap of reins, the mud wagon pulled away, disappearing into the night.

"I'm in here, ma'am," the bearded man said. He watched Molly pick up her valise and come to the door. "Name's Joe Orley."

"I'm Molly Owens," she said. Reaching the doorway, she added, "I need overnight accommodations, and a horse tomorrow. I understand you have saddle horses for hire."

"Yep," he said. He backed into the station and held the door open for her.

Molly stepped in and saw four men playing cards at a round table near the middle of the small room. The men turned and looked at her.

Orley said, "The room will run four dollars, ma'am."

Molly set her valise down, seeing the card players exchange glances as this exorbitant rate was quoted. They were a strange lot, young and dressed as cowhands, but Molly sensed they were not locals. All were armed, and two of the men had extra cartridge belts slung across the backs of their chairs.

Molly turned to Joe Orley. "That includes a hot bath and a pitcher of water in the room, doesn't it?"

The men at the table guffawed, and Molly turned to see Orley's face redden. He was a potbellied man, and his salt-and-pepper beard gave a gray cast to his face.

"Why, sure, ma'am," he muttered. "I'll get the room ready."

After he left, one of the men at the table said, "Sit yourself down, lady. Do you play cards?"

Molly saw that the speaker was a brown-haired young man with a full mustache. He grinned, showing a missing front tooth, and held up a glass of whiskey to her.

"You men look like you could skin a Mississippi riverboat gambler," Molly said, bringing a laugh from them.

"We're just having us a friendly game," he said.

Molly smiled, but shook her head.

"You aim to stay a spell," he asked, "or passing through?"

Molly heard a note of forced sincerity in the young man's voice. He pretended to make polite conversation, but he wanted more.

Molly shook her head again and turned away. By lantern light she saw a portrait of a nude woman on the wall over a small bar. Lying provocatively on her side with one plump hand on her hip, the naked woman stared back with a faint smile at anyone who gazed at her.

"Now we've got two pretty ladies in the room," the young man said, "and one's real. Boy, is she ever real."

Molly did not acknowledge the remark. Moments later Joe Orley returned. He took Molly to her room near the end of a short hall. True to his word, a small tub of hot water was there.

"Thank you, Mr. Orley," Molly said.

He grinned sheepishly at her, his eyes lingering on her for a moment, then turned and left. Molly closed the door, noticing there was no lock on it.

The room was sparsely furnished. A narrow bunk with a thin mattress was near the far wall, and at the foot of it stood a table and chair. A lamp was there, along with a bucket of water and a threadbare towel. Molly went to the table and held up the lamp. She saw insects swimming on the water's surface.

Molly secured the door as best she could by wedging the rickety chair under the handle. Laying her Colt .38 on the bed, she blew out the lamp and undressed in the dark. She had decided to bathe in darkness. The walls of the room were whipsawn planks, full of knotholes, and she had the uncomfortable feeling she was being watched.

After the bath, Molly lay under a scratchy and smelly wool blanket on the bunk. Her companion tonight was the revolver in her hand. She closed her eyes, just now realizing how weary she was.

Small sounds came from far away, soft scrapes that might have been part of a dream. The dream became real when a rough hand covered her mouth and pushed down, hard.

"Don't say nothing, and you won't get cut."

Molly felt the point of a knife at her throat, realizing too late that the intruder had eased open the door while she slept.

CHAPTER VII

Suddenly awake and alert, Molly discovered that the revolver had slipped from her grasp during the night, and now she groped for it.

"Don't move, I told you."

The point of the knife pricked her neck, and Molly lay still. The man threw the blanket aside. In one swift motion he ripped her flannel nightgown from her body. He ran a rough hand over her breasts and groped downward.

"You don't need that," Molly whispered.

"Huh?"

Molly raised one hand and brought her fingertips to the knife blade. "Put that away, and come to me. I want you."

"You want me?"

"Yes," Molly whispered.

A long moment passed. "The easy way doesn't do it for me. You gotta fight. Fight back."

Molly had hoped to deceive her attacker by pretending to relent. Once the knife was away from her throat, she was prepared to punch his windpipe or drive her knee into his scrotum.

"Fight, or I'll cut you open."

Molly raised her hand up the length of the knife blade to the man's hand. First she touched a stub, and then three fingers clutching the handle. The man was missing his little finger.

"Fight!"

Molly feigned struggling, writhing and slapping her hands against her attacker's upper body. He was shirtless, and her blows slapped loudly against his skin. Warm moisture ran down her neck.

"You're cutting me!"

Molly now struggled in earnest against his pressing weight. He grasped her wrists, pinning her arms down while jabbing his knee between her legs.

Molly reacted both from instinctive rage and from her training in self-defense. She kicked a leg up, banged her foot against his body, then raised her head, turned, and sank her teeth into his hairy forearm.

The man cried out. He tried to pull back, but Molly clamped her jaw shut. With his free hand, he released her wrist and struck the side of her head with a panicky, vicious blow.

Her ears ringing, Molly felt her attacker's weight shift. She let go of his arm and shoved. The man slid off the bed.

Molly leaped off the bunk, seeing the shadowy form hunched on the floor. She lashed out with her foot, the heel of it striking his side. He groaned but struggled to his feet. Molly came in low, driving her fist into his abdomen. The man doubled over and lurched for the door.

Molly rushed to the bunk, frantically searching for her revolver. Behind, she was aware of the door opening. The gun was not in the blanket, and by the time she found it under the bunk—where it must have fallen during the night—her attacker was gone.

Breathing hard, Molly looked out into the empty hallway. Then she closed the door and made her way to the lamp on the table. Matches were there, and she struck one. She touched the flame to the wick and turned around. Pale light from the lamp wavered against the plank walls.

Her valise had tumbled over, spilling out clothes as the intruder must have kicked it, and the chair lay on its side across the room. Molly picked up the chair and wedged it under the door handle again. Then she picked up her clothes.

Her attacker had left his trousers behind. Molly went through the pockets but found nothing. The trousers were cotton, a common type, and gave no clue to the man's identity.

Feeling another droplet of moisture on her neck, Molly rummaged through her valise and found her hand mirror. She looked at her reflection by lamplight. The cut on her neck was not deep. She dipped a handkerchief into the bucket of water on the table and wiped the cut clean.

Molly blew out the lamp and lay down on the bunk. Her anger was slowly replaced by fear. She had been close to death, and now that reality loomed large in the dark room. After daylight she opened her eyes, surprised that she had been able to sleep.

She dressed in her riding clothes, feeling sore from the attack and groggy from lack of sleep. She wore a denim divided skirt, light cotton blouse, and a new ladies' Stetson, tan in color. She finished dressing by knotting a kerchief around her neck, covering the superficial wound.

Molly left the room with her valise in hand. She walked down the short hall, still feeling angry, but she took some consolation in the fact that her attacker had begged her to resist, and she had given him more fight than he could handle.

Molly ate a hearty breakfast of scrambled eggs and ham slices. She sat at the round table where the card players had been last night. Those four men were nowhere to be seen this morning, and Molly decided not to ask Joe Orley about them or other men who might have stayed overnight.

She had another investigation in front of her, and lodging a complaint with the county sheriff would only delay her and might raise some questions she'd prefer not to answer.

Orley himself was not her attacker. Molly had confirmed that when the man had entered the room carrying a platter of scrambled eggs and ham in one hand and a cup of steaming coffee in the other. He had all ten fingers.

"I want to hire a saddle horse," Molly reminded Orley after breakfast, "and I want to buy some canteens and tins of food."

Orley looked at her for a long moment before replying. "You figure on taking a ride into the desert?"

Molly nodded.

"Alone?"

"That's right," Molly said.

He shook his head. "Taking a horse into that wild country is a risky business. If you don't know where to find the few water holes . . . well, I'll lose a good horse."

Molly smiled. "I do appreciate your concern for your horses, Mr. Orley." She reached into her handbag and drew out five twenty-dollar gold pieces. "Here's a deposit for a good horse and saddle. I'll pay cash for the supplies I need. Now, Mr. Orley, are we going to do business?"

The pudgy innkeeper grinned. "Yes, ma'am, we'll do business. We sure will."

CHAPTER VIII

Under the midmorning sun Molly rode out of the Wild Horse stage station on a wiry sorrel. Four two-quart canteens were tied to the saddle, and a canvas sack of supplies was strapped behind the cantle.

Aware that Orley watched her leave, Molly followed the stage road south. She did not think the innkeeper would trail her, but she did not want to make it easy for him to tell anyone else where she had gone.

Straight ahead, fifty miles distant, black peaks of the Henry Mountains rose up. She had read about those lonely mountains. Largely unexplored, the mountain range had not been discovered until 1869. They were the last to be put on the map of the United States.

Molly rode toward the Henry Mountains for half an hour, when she topped a small rise. On the other side she dropped out of sight of the Wild Horse stage station and turned the sorrel to the east. No one followed.

She pulled her Stetson down against the harsh and hot glare of the morning sun and rode into the desert. Just under the blazing sun, thirty miles away, stood the stone formations of the famous Robbers Roost.

Orley undoubtedly suspected that was her destination, but Molly had been careful not to confirm his unspoken guess. If he knew, he might send a warning to outlaws in the Roost.

The card players in his station last night were very likely men on the run, outlaws who had either come out of the "City of Refuge" or were on their way in. Hunted men could hide there as long as money and food held out, and after several weeks could come out and ride for a region where they could pass unrecognized.

The air grew increasingly hot as Molly rode into the rising sun. Sweat trickled down her back, and already her mouth was dry. She reined up and swung down. She poured water into her Stetson and let the horse drink, and took a precious swallow from the canteen herself.

The distant formations of red stone were huge, rising up out of the barren desert several hundred feet. Cracked into enormous blocks, narrow canyons ran between them in a maze. Molly stepped into the saddle and rode on, wondering now if she could possibly find the one canyon that led into the Roost.

The land here was as barren as any she'd ever seen. Prickly pear grew in small clumps, along with desert sage. The sage leaves, silver-blue in color, were very small. Small leaves conserved moisture. By contrast Molly thought of the lush growth in the mountain valley where Buck had lived with the old hermit. There, the leaves of plants were full and thick beside the running creek, and the colors were rich.

The only wildlife Molly saw were lizards skittering from one patch of shade to another, a few tiny birds perched on sage branches, and a small rattlesnake sliding through stubby grass. Other desert creatures were here, Molly thought, as she guided the horse in a wide berth around the rattlesnake, but would not venture out in the heat of day. They had better sense.

After watering the horse at noon, Molly sat in his shadow and opened a can of pears. She thirstily drank the sweet juice, then ate the fruit. After resting, she rode on toward the massive stone formations.

The wiry sorrel was evidently at home in this hot climate. His head did not droop, and his tail switched lazily as he plodded steadily eastward. Molly's clothes were dampened by sweat, and she had the sensation that she was losing water almost as fast as she could consume it.

Throughout the afternoon she stopped frequently and poured water into her Stetson for the horse. Riding on, the wet hat on her head felt good, but quickly dried out in the blazing sun.

Molly caught sight of a water hole at sundown. In the vast brown-and-gray landscape, her eye was caught by a patch of green grass. The horse either saw it, too, or caught a scent of water, for he turned and walked straight to the small oasis.

The pool of water was surrounded by moist ground. In the mud Molly saw hundreds of animal tracks, from delicate imprints of birds to the split hoofprints of deer. She dismounted and let the horse drink, then knelt beside the pool and lifted a handful of water to her lips. The water was bitter.

At sundown the desert air quickly cooled. The land did, too, like a frying pan taken off a campfire. Molly made camp near the spring, eating jerked venison and another can of fruit. She drank sparingly from the canteen rather than from the spring water.

In the mud around the pool, Molly saw a few tracks left by shod horses. None were fresh, and there was no sign of human tracks. The hoofprints might have been made by ranch horses gone wild. Wild horses roamed this desert, and Molly gave up the idea of trying to track the hoofprints leading away from this spring.

As the evening light thinned, she looked up at the towering cliffs. They were only a few miles away now, stretching out north to south as far as she could see. She was eager to explore the canyons, but knew she must conserve her horse's strength.

The sun had dropped like a stone, and as darkness closed in, Molly hobbled the sorrel and then spread out her blankets. She lay down, using her folded clothes as a pillow, and looked up at the starry sky.

To the east the black sky was cleaved by the high cliffs, an ominous shape in the silent night.

In the morning she got an early start and rode south several miles before the sun came up. The air quickly heated, and she began to perspire even though she now rode in the shadow of the great sandstone formations.

She searched the ground for signs of horses and men, but found nothing. Riding to the mouths of several narrow canyons that penetrated the towering cliffs, Molly could see that none of these were used by horsebackers.

Soon convinced that her search had gone in the wrong direction, Molly turned back. She stopped at the spring and let the sorrel drink while she opened a can of sardines. After eating them with crackers, she mounted and rode along the base of the cliffs northward.

The sun bore down relentlessly. The hot glare pressed against her like a deadly weight, a weight that sapped her strength. She watched the ground intently, but the heat of the day made her lightheaded. Her thoughts wandered. She began reliving the past.

She was a scrawny teenage girl with a girl's worries about her figure, boys, and a recent spat with her best friend. That hot summer afternoon was a vivid memory after all these years.

She'd answered the knock on the door of her family's home in Philadelphia to find a pair of grim-faced men standing on the porch, hats in hand. They brought the first news of the railroad accident that had killed her mother and father.

As crushing as that reality had been, Molly now knew that it had hastened her transformation from girlhood to womanhood. In the following weeks she argued and fought for the right of her brother to stay with her rather than be sent off to a foster home. She'd won the battle, and the two of them had finished their growing-up years in the home of a neighbor lady.

Chick. That was the pet name of her brother, and memories of him seeped into Molly's mind as she rode northward through the Utah desert. The sorrel plodded along, the rhythm of his movements almost hypnotic. Molly remembered that after her brother's graduation from high school, he had packed his belongings, put on his new hat, and left the East to fulfill his lifelong dream of going "out West."

Those two words had come from Chick's mouth countless times, and when Molly last hugged him, they both had cried, shedding tears of sorrow and happiness.

She never saw him again. In the time she had been trained as an operative for the Fenton Investigative Agency, her brother had worked on several ranches in Colorado. Molly was stationed in Denver, and she and her brother kept in touch through sporadic correspondence, both living the lives they had chosen for themselves.

After learning of his murder in a small town near the ranch where Chick had worked as a cowhand, Molly had gone there immediately. Her investigation uncovered a land dispute, and the fact that her brother had been killed by a rogue town marshal. Molly solved the case and brought the killer to justice.

A female shriek and high-pitched laughter brought Molly out of her reverie. She reined up, just now realizing she'd ridden into a barren hollow at the base of a high, sheer cliff of red sandstone. The laughter had come from the other side of the low hill in front of her.

Molly shook herself awake and dismounted. Taking her field glasses out of a saddlebag, she strode up the sloping hill. Near the top she dropped to her knees and eased ahead until she could see over it. What she saw might have come from a bizarre dream or a mirage.

CHAPTER IX

This was no mirage, but as Molly raised the field glasses to her eyes and brought the heavily loaded wagon into focus, she could hardly believe what she saw.

The freight wagon, loaded with a pair of water barrels and boxes of supplies, was pulled by two white draft horses. The team was driven by a woman, and beside her sat another woman, who was talking and laughing gaily. She held a pink parasol over their heads.

The pair were dressed in high style, wearing full and frilly white dresses, and their musical voices carried across the silent desert, punctuated by bursts of hysterical, perhaps drunken laughter. Molly followed their progress, and through the field glasses she saw the wagon disappear into a narrow canyon.

Molly got to her feet and hurried back to the sorrel. She swung up into the saddle and rode over the top of the rise. Following the wagon tracks, she saw other hoofprints leading into the canyon.

Molly rode into the canyon and continued through the narrow passageway for half a mile until she heard echoing laughter from the women. She reined up. The wagon traveled slowly, and she did not want to overtake it.

While she waited, Molly looked up at the towering walls of sandstone on her right and her left. The cliffs were delicately inscribed with dark vertical streaks, decorations left by spring rains and melting snows over tens of thousands of years.

The walls closed off the world, all but a bright patch of sky overhead, and while this land had a strange beauty, Molly felt a growing sense of powerlessness and insignificance. Despite the oppressive heat, a shiver ran up her back.

A quarter of an hour later, she rode on, trying to shake off the sense of isolation. A mile farther, the canyon rounded a sharp turn, one of many here, and divided. Twin trails left by the iron-tired wagon led into the canyon on her right, and Molly followed them.

This canyon was scarcely wider than a freight wagon. Sheer cliffs rose up several hundred feet on either side, like a great vise. Molly followed the twisting path of this canyon for more than an hour, losing all sense of direction.

Along the way, more canyons broke off from this one. Becoming lost in this enormous maze was a living nightmare. Molly knew she could wander for days without finding her way out. She was glad she had the wagon tracks to follow, even though she did not know where they would lead her.

The heat was stifling, radiating off the sandstone cliffs as though they were the sides of an oven. Molly drank from her canteen. She had consumed more than half of her water supply and realized that if she had not found the spring where the sorrel drank his fill, her water would be long gone. Even so, she had deprived herself and was becoming light-headed.

The canyon opened, and other small canyons led away from this one like spokes of a wheel. The trail left by the wagon showed the way into a wider canyon straight ahead, beyond a jumble of fallen rock.

Molly rode around the rocks and saw that the canyon where the wagon had gone led to open ground. The moment she reined up to peer ahead, a man came out from behind the rocks.

"Git off'n that horse."

Startled, Molly looked at him. He waved a shotgun

at her, and she obeyed. The man was squat, dressed in dirty clothes and a battered hat with a wide brim.

"What do we got here?" he said, coming toward her.

Molly saw him level the shotgun at her, and she smiled. "Just a lady out for a ride in the desert."

"Don't give me no smart talk," he said, stopping one pace away from her. He looked back the way she had come. "Who'd you bring with you?"

"No one," Molly said, sliding a hand across her breasts toward the revolver holstered under her jacket. "I'm here to see Cole Estes."

He swung his gaze to her. "Cole Estes," he repeated.

"I have business with him," Molly said. She added, "A private matter."

"The hell," he said. Still suspicious that she was not alone, he turned away and looked back.

Molly saw her moment. She drew her Colt .38 in a swift motion, and lunged, pressing the gun against his ear. "Drop that shotgun, mister."

He swore, but obeyed. The shotgun clattered to the ground. Molly quickly searched him for a handgun and found a sheathed knife on his belt. She tossed it away.

"All right," Molly said, backing up a step, "take me in."

"Huh?" he said.

She gestured with her revolver. "Your camp is just ahead, isn't it? Take me there." When he did not move, she lowered the gun and aimed at his leg. "Don't make me shoot."

He swore again, and turned away. He strode toward the passageway that led to the open ground where the freight wagon had gone. Molly swung up into the saddle and followed.

The canyon opened out to a wide bowl that was half a mile or more in diameter. Most of the land here was barren, but across the way at the base of sandstone cliffs Molly saw a patch of green grass and a cedar thicket. A glint of water caught her eye.

Beside this tiny oasis stood three large white tents, a canvas lean-to, and the loaded freight wagon. In the shade of the lean-to, near the spring, stood ten or twelve horses, switching their tails.

Halfway across the open ground Molly heard shrill laughter and a merry shriek. But as she rode closer, a man's urgent voice came to her, and moments later the flap of the nearest tent was thrown open.

Three men came out, guns drawn. They were soon followed by three others who came out of a second tent. Behind them, Molly saw the two women poke their heads out.

A dozen yards away, Molly reined up. The gunmen spread out, aiming their revolvers at Molly. One was hatless. His reddish hair gleamed in the sunlight. He was the one who spoke. "Poor odds for a shoot-out, ma'am."

Molly holstered her Colt .38. "I didn't come here to trade lead, but this man forced my hand."

The bearded man looked around sheepishly.

"Lenny was only doing what he was told," the man said, squinting against the sun's glare as he came forward.

Molly said, "You're Cole Estes, aren't you?"

He paused. "I don't believe I know you."

"You don't," Molly said.

"You act like we've met," he said.

"I see a family resemblance," Molly said. "Your son looks a lot like you."

CHAPTER X

Cole Estes was a lean and powerful-looking man with a sharp, hawklike expression. Now, as the five gunmen turned to look at him, Estes stared at Molly in a long moment of silence.

"You'd better climb down," he said at last. Turning to the men, he quietly ordered them to return to the tents. Then he told Lenny to go back to his guard post.

Molly dismounted, seeing Lenny cast an angry look at her as he passed by.

"Come into my tent," Cole Estes said, taking the reins of Molly's horse, "and we'll get out of this heat."

Molly walked beside him as they followed the men back to the tents. She looked around at the sandstone cliffs ringing Robbers Roost. It was a natural fortress, but as she had seen, the Roost was only as secure as the guard made it. Of the gunmen, Molly had recognized only two others. Matt Bledsoe and Pony Diehl matched the descriptions she'd read in the files of the Denver U.S. marshal's office.

Cole Estes led the sorrel to the spring and then took Molly to the nearest tent. He pulled the flap open and stepped aside for her.

Molly took off her Stetson and ducked in. An odor of hot canvas filled her nostrils. She straightened up and saw one cot, saddles and gear, and a few boxes of food. On the cot was a gray hat.

Estes moved behind her and snatched the hat off the cot. "Sit down," he said. He pulled a wooden box up, turned it on its end, and sat down. "Damned if I've ever met a woman like you. Who are you?"

"My name is Molly Owens," she said. "I'm an operative for the Fenton Investigative Agency."

"And you figure on collecting that Union Pacific reward on me, right?" he asked.

"No," Molly said. "I came to deliver a message from your son."

"Lady, I don't have a son," he said.

"Birth records prove otherwise," Molly said. She added, "So do my own eyes. He does look a lot like you."

Cole Estes winced. "All right, I may have sired a child, but I was hardly more than a boy myself. I was never a father to him."

"You may not think of him as your son," Molly said, "but that doesn't mean he's going to forget about you. In fact, just the opposite is true. He's very curious about you."

"What're you driving at?" he asked.

"He wants to see you," Molly said.

Cole's eyes widened.

"The boy wants to look at you, talk to you," Molly explained. "He wants to know who you are."

"Damn," Cole whispered, looking away. "A man can't get away from the past . . ." His voice trailed off.

"Do you want to?" Molly asked.

He met her gaze. "Everyone does, Miss Owens. Everyone wants to leave the past behind, forgotten."

"But you say it can't be done?" she asked.

A faint smile came into his expression. "Nope." He looked at her with renewed interest. "Well, tell me about the kid. How old is he?"

"Fourteen," Molly said. She described her encounter with the grizzly bear in the Colorado Rockies and told him how Buck had saved her life. She went on to tell what she had found out about him after their return to Denver.

Cole listened intently, a somber expression coming

to his face while she spoke. His eyes took on an empty stare, as though he was peering into his own past. Molly judged that he did not like what he saw.

"Cole?" a man called from outside the tent. "We still got us a horse race?"

The spell was broken as Cole Estes blinked and looked toward the closed flap of the tent. "Sure, we do, Billy," he said. "Get that wind-broke plug of yours ready for a run."

He stood, looking down at Molly. He seemed ready to say something, but then he turned and moved to the end of the tent. Over his shoulder he said, "Come outside, Miss Owens, and you'll see me make a believer out of a man who thinks he owns a fast horse."

Molly followed Cole out of the tent into a blaze of sunlight. She put on her Stetson and pulled the brim down against the glare, glancing at the sun hovering over the rim of the cliffs to the west.

"Here you go, Cole."

Molly saw the small man she had recognized as Pony Diehl bring a cream-colored quarter horse to Cole. He was a wiry, fine-featured man, now unarmed, wearing pin-striped trousers, a dress shirt with no collar, and expensive boots.

A short distance away stood a bigger man, well-dressed, too, who looked on with bemused interest. He was Matt Bledsoe, ruggedly handsome with a neatly trimmed mustache.

"Billy, where are you?" Cole called out after he had swung up into the saddle.

From behind the canvas lean-to near the spring came a half-wild brown-and-white horse ridden by the man Molly assumed was Billy Truax. The other gunmen were members of his gang. All were unclean with ragged beards.

Billy Truax sawed back on the reins of his skittish horse. Wide-eyed, the animal bore scars on his neck and shoulders from fights, and now he was looking for open ground.

Molly stepped back with Pony Diehl as the horses

were positioned. The half-wild one stretched his neck out and tried to bite Cole's horse on the rump. The quarter horse reared.

"Get that desert scrub away," Cole shouted, bringing his horse down.

Pony said, "You'd better run this race before those horses kill each other."

Molly heard Matt Bledsoe chuckle, but when she turned to look at him and their eyes met, his smile faded.

"Get us going!" Cole shouted.

One of Truax's gunmen casually drew his revolver and fired it into the sky.

Both horses bolted. All the men whooped as the two powerful animals galloped away, running stride for stride across the flat. A cloud of dust churned up behind them.

The two horsemen became ghostly figures in the haze of red dust. Molly could not tell who was ahead but knew the race was close when she saw them turn and come back. The drumming hooves grew louder. Out of the dust now, Molly saw Cole leaning over his horse's neck, a beautiful sight of man and horse together, moving with great power and speed. A dozen yards behind came the brown-and-white horse, plunging at an ungainly but fast pace.

"Whip that plug!" shouted a member of Billy's gang. "Whip him!" The two women joined with their shrieks.

"You've got him, Cole!" Pony called.

The cream-colored quarter horse thundered toward the tents at full gallop. Twenty yards away, Cole straightened up and raised an arm in a gesture of victory as the horse circled away from the tents. Truax gave up the race and came in at a trot.

Cole circled around and joined him. "That jughead has power, Billy, but no style."

The outlaw grinned. "Not bad for a desert horse that's only been wearing a saddle for a few days. Wait'll I work him awhile."

"Then we'll run again," Cole said. He turned to the

men grouped around them. "Gentlemen, I believe you owe me some money."

The two women crowded around Truax after he dismounted, chattering and assuring him he would win next time. After the bets were settled and the horses tended, Cole took Molly aside.

"I've thought it over, Miss Owens," he said, "and I've decided it's too late for me to start being a father to that boy now. Nothing good would come of it if I tried."

"Is that what you want me to tell him?" Molly asked.

Cole paused, looking out across the flat. The sun was down, but the air was hot and still. "I reckon so." He thought a moment. "Tell him a man's got to live by his own decisions. I have since I was sixteen or so. Only, I hope that boy makes better decisions than I did, Miss Owens—"

"Call me Molly," she said.

He cast a long look at her. "All right."

They stood together in silence, with the only sounds coming from the Truax gang and the women in one of the tents.

"You'll never make it out of the Roost before dark," Cole said. "I could show you the way out of the canyon country this evening, but you'd have to make a night crossing to Wild Horse or Greenriver."

"The sorrel would never make it," Molly said.

Cole nodded. "Joe Orley's plug, isn't it?"

"Yes," Molly said. "He's better than a plug."

Cole grinned at her. "Every horse I don't own is a plug, Molly." He turned to the tents. "Tonight you can use my cot. I'll bunk with Matt and Pony. Now, let's go see what Effie and Alice have scorched for supper."

CHAPTER XI

Molly was impressed by how well supplied the outlaws were. The third tent was a combination dining hall, gambling parlor, and saloon. Besides being well stocked with expensive bottles of whiskey and straw-packed crates of champagne, the tent was equipped with a military-style camp stove, folding tables and chairs, and boxes of food.

After a meal of steaks, thick slices of fresh bread, cooked vegetables, and fruit, the outlaws gathered around the table for a poker game. Each man dipped into bank money bags and drew out handfuls of twenty- and fifty-dollar gold pieces. Cole invited Molly to sit in.

"This game's too rich for me," she said.

Cole laughed. "Don't be fooled by all this money. We're just using it to pass the time of day. At the end of the game it all goes back into the sacks. We'll divide it up when we ride out." He looked at her and added, "It's hard enough to stay friendly in this Roost without a man losing his loot in a poker game. We'd kill each other if we played for keeps."

"The same rule doesn't apply to horse racing, I take it," Molly said.

Cole chuckled as the cards were dealt. "Horse racing is a serious business. We placed bets with the money we had in our pockets." He looked at Molly. "I won a grand total of twelve dollars."

Throughout the evening Molly noted that Cole ruled this Roost with a quiet authority. All the men and the two women deferred to him. But he alone was friendly to her. Effie and Alice ignored her, and the others seemed to think she was Cole's woman. Matt Bledsoe was outright unfriendly to her.

Molly left the tent and walked out into the gathering darkness. The air had cooled. She walked to the cedars that grew around the spring and caught the strong scent of water. Looking back toward the tents, she was struck by the fact that from outward appearances the outlaw stronghold could have been a typical camp in the wilderness. It was as peaceful and serene as a camp of hunters or any other group on an excursion into the desert.

The third tent glowed from lanterns within, and while Molly stood there watching, she saw the flap open. Cole came out. He looked around, then came toward her.

"Molly?"

"Over here," she answered.

Cole came to her and stood beside her. "What're you thinking?"

"I was noticing how quiet and peaceful it is out here," she said. "And how good the water smells."

"This desert makes you appreciate water, for a fact," Cole said. "It's peaceful, all right, but after a few weeks the damned silence can drive you mad."

"Is that why you keep the men busy with horse races, card games, and women?" Molly asked.

"Not the women," Cole replied in a sharp tone of voice. "I don't believe in having women in camp. Matt and Pony and I never have. Women can lead to trouble. I tried to tell Billy that we'll have plenty of time for romance when we ride out, but he wouldn't go along."

Now Molly understood why Matt Bledsoe had been so unfriendly to her. The Estes and Truax gangs had more of a truce than a partnership, and their union was not an easy one.

Cole said, "When I asked what you were thinking, I had an idea you might have a low opinion of me after what I said about seeing the boy."

Molly turned to him. In the faint light of evening, Cole Estes was a shadowy figure, but even so she sensed the strength of his presence. After tomorrow she expected never to see him again and was surprised that he was concerned about what she thought of him.

"I don't have a low opinion of you, Cole," she said. "Perhaps I should turn the question to you. What are you thinking?"

Cole did not reply immediately. Molly heard the sound of a horse stamping his hoof in the canvas lean-to, and then laughter and a shriek came from the tent where a new card game was in progress.

"A lot of memories come crowding in," Cole murmured. "I wasn't much more than a boy myself . . ." His voice trailed off. "Hell, there's no need to dig all that up again."

"If you did," Molly said, "your son would know more about his past."

"So he can spend the rest of his life trying to get away from it?" Cole asked.

"No," Molly said, "so he can understand himself a little better."

Cole paused. "That's a tall order."

"If you stood face to face with your son," Molly said, "the order might not seem so tall."

"Maybe you're right," Cole said. He exhaled loudly. "Right now I need a drink. Will you join me?"

Molly shook her head. She knew she would not be welcomed in that tent, and she was tired.

"I'll turn in," she said. "I've got a long, hot ride in front of me tomorrow."

Molly lay awake on the cot that night, her mind racing with conflicting thoughts and memories. She thought of the pursuing grizzly bear and of Buck saving her life. Thoughts of her brother came into her mind, and she wondered why.

Unaccountably, she found herself thinking of Cole Estes, of standing near him in the darkness outside.

He was an appealing man, both strong and vulnerable, with a leader's air of loneliness.

She drifted into sleep feeling a desire for him. At daybreak she was abruptly awakened by distant gunfire, and from the next tent came screams of men and women in agony.

CHAPTER XII

Molly instinctively rolled off the cot onto the ground. Another volley of gunfire shattered the early-morning silence, followed by more screams and shouts.

"My God!"

"They've come to murder us!"

A moment later there was another eruption of rifle fire from somewhere out on the open ground. Horses squealed in pain.

"The bastards are killing the horses!"

Molly hugged the ground at the next blast of gunfire. Bullets whispered through the tent, thunking into tent poles, tearing at the blankets on the empty cot, and raising plumes of dirt around her. After the volley she glanced around and saw holes stitched in the canvas walls.

She snatched her handbag from the cot and crawled to the rear of the tent. Reaching into the tooled leather handbag, she drew out her barlow knife, opened the blade, and slashed the canvas.

Outside, Molly crawled away from the tent toward the sparse protection offered by the cedars around the spring. Ahead, she glimpsed movement, and for a moment feared she was moving toward more attackers.

But then she recognized Cole. Dressed in his underwear, he raised up behind a cedar and frantically waved at her to come.

He flopped down to the ground at the sound of more rifle fire. Molly lay still, hearing lead slap into stone. The cliffs beyond the tents were peppered with bullets.

Molly crawled the rest of the way to the spring when the rifles were silent, joining Cole behind a gnarled cedar. A short distance away, Matt Bledsoe lay on the stubby grass at the back edge of the spring, a revolver in his hand.

Molly turned and saw Pony Diehl stretched out in the water, the backside of his nude body above the surface. Propped on his elbows, he aimed a long-barreled Winchester out toward the open ground beyond the tents. The rifle was equipped with a telescopic sight, and Diehl peered into it, his fingers pressing against the trigger.

While she watched, the rifle bucked against Diehl's shoulder, and the roar of the big shoulder weapon reverberated through her ears.

Pony looked back over his shoulder at Cole. "Four of them, better'n a hundred yards away. They're behind rocks or something."

Matt said, "Want me to get my rifle and set up a crossfire?"

Cole shook his head. "Stay put, Matt, or they'll gun us down like they did Billy and the others. Pony, can you get them?"

Pony Diehl looked through the telescopic sight again. "I see one of them now."

"Take him out," Cole said. He edged closer to Molly and put an arm over her shoulders. "You all right?"

Molly nodded, just as another volley of gunfire erupted. She hugged the ground, realizing that four men were out there with repeating rifles. When the guns were empty, the men would reload and cut loose again. They had chosen their targets well. None of the horses were standing, and Molly heard no sounds from the other tents.

When the volley stopped, Pony fired. "Got one," he said. He was up to his elbows in mud, peering past a gnarled cedar. "Saw the top of his head come off."

He fired again and jacked a fresh round into the

chamber. Another shot, and Pony said triumphant-
ly, "Two down!"

Cole edged into the water for a clearer view. "Matt,
let them know we're here."

Both men aimed their revolvers toward the open
ground and fired rapidly. The range was too long, but
the message was clear.

Pony fired again, then raised up. "They're running!
The bastards are running!"

Molly lifted her head and saw two men with rifles
running toward the canyon. Pony took aim and fired.
One of the men tumbled to the ground, rifle flying
from his hand. A second shot from Pony's Winchester
dropped the other man. Both lay on the ground, still.

"Some shooting, Pony," Matt said, getting to his
feet.

"Better hold tight," Cole said. "Might be more of
them."

Bledsoe knelt, and Pony sat down in the water at
the far edge of the spring, watching. Minutes dragged
past in complete silence as the morning light brightened. The eastern sky turned red.

"Who were they?" Molly asked in a low voice.

Cole shrugged as he looked out through the cedars.
"U.P. detectives or bounty hunters."

Molly looked at the tents. One was nearly shred-
ded. That was the tent occupied by the Truax gang
and Effie and Alice.

Half an hour had slowly passed when Cole got to
his feet. Bledsoe, dressed only in underwear, too,
stood up. He moved around the spring and went to
the tents. Molly heard him curse as he looked into
one.

A splash of water drew her attention to the spring.
She saw Pony raise up out of the water. Naked, his
lean body was gleaming white. With his long rifle in
hand, he stepped gingerly out of the spring and walked
through the cedars to the tent where Matt Bledsoe
stood.

"Damn," Pony said, pulling open the flap. "They must have stood up when the shooting started."

Molly got to her feet and gathered her nightgown around her. She followed Cole toward that tent and got close enough to see a tangle of bodies streaked with blood. They were scantily clad, some nude, and as Molly looked through the flap that Pony held open, she saw strawberry-blond hair.

"We're riding out of here," Cole said softly.

"How?" Pony asked, releasing the tent flap. He turned around, seemingly unaware of his nudity. "The bastards gunned down our horses."

Molly saw a grim expression on Cole's face. His cream-colored quarter horse was among the dead horses in the canvas lean-to.

"They rode in on horses," Cole said, looking out at the bodies of the attackers. "We'll use theirs."

Molly looked out there and saw that the riflemen had piled stones up for fortifications. They must have done that work during the night and observed the tents. Their main target had been the tent where lanterns blazed much of the night.

"What about Lenny?" Pony asked. "Was he on guard last night?"

Matt Bledsoe said, "Get some clothes on, Pony. We'll go have a look and see if we can find the horses." When Pony moved away, Bledsoe said to Cole, "I reckon those killers followed her in here."

Molly realized he meant her. She watched the two men regard one another.

"That isn't the way I figure it," Cole said.

Bledsoe clenched his jaw. "No women in camp—isn't that what you always said?"

Cole nodded, not taking his eyes off his longtime partner. "That's right, Matt. And I'm remembering how Molly found her way into the Roost."

"How was that?" Bledsoe asked.

"She followed that damned freight wagon Billy insisted on bringing in," Cole said.

Bledsoe's jaw jutted out. "Well, like I said, it's women that caused this."

"But not this woman," Cole said. He added, "Hell, Matt, you're right. Truax never should have let those women into the Roost. But it was part of the deal when he helped us stop the U.P. train."

Bledsoe grunted. "I want to see who those killers are." He turned and strode away from the tents toward the crude breastworks of stone. He was followed by Pony Diehl, who had pulled on his trousers and boots.

Molly went into the tent she had slept in last night. She slumped down on the cot, feeling sick and exhausted. The tension and terror of the last hour had drained her, and the carnage, so sudden and strangely casual, had left her sickened.

She dressed and packed her valise, then lay down on the cot and rested. Presently she heard horses and voices outside. Bledsoe reported that the guard at the mouth of the canyon, Lenny, was dead. His throat had been slit.

Molly stepped out of the tent in time to hear Matt Bledsoe tell Cole about the attackers. "Never seen them before," he said. "They weren't carrying badges, so I figure they're bounty hunters. One was missing a finger."

Molly saw that Matt and Pony had brought back four saddle horses and two pack animals. The man transferred the sacks of coins to the backs of the pack animals and filled all their canteens with water.

As they rode out, Molly reined up at the fortifications. She dismounted and examined the bodies of the four attackers.

"You know them?" Bledsoe asked accusingly.

Molly saw the corpse of the young man who had flirted with her at the Wild Horse station. He was missing the little finger of his right hand, and now she knew he was the man who had tried to rape her that night. The others were the men she'd seen at the poker table.

Molly climbed up into the saddle before she answered Bledsoe's question. The three men turned in their saddles, looking back at her.

"They were in Joe Orley's place two nights ago," Molly said.

CHAPTER XIII

They rode out of the canyon lands and crossed the open desert, reaching the Wild Horse stage station after midnight. They watered the horses by starlight and turned them out in the corral. Spurs ringing on the plank porch, the men entered the stage station and called for Joe Orley. Molly came in behind them.

Orley came down the narrow hall, carrying a lamp. His shadow danced at his feet, and he seemed sleepy and groggy until he raised the lamp and saw that the woman with the outlaws was Molly. He stopped at the edge of the room and regarded them with unconcealed surprise.

"Bring that sorrel back, did you?" he asked.

Before Molly could reply, Cole said, "We had some trouble in the Roost. Billy's gang was shot to pieces, along with the women. We buried them out there."

"Be damned," Orley muttered, lowering the lamp so that his heavily jowled face fell into shadow.

"Lost our horses to the murdering bastards, too," Cole went on. "Your sorrel went down."

Orley swore, then slowly turned toward Molly. "I reckon I'll be keeping that deposit."

"How much?" Cole asked. When Joe Orley did not answer, he turned to Molly.

"A hundred dollars," she said.

Cole turned back to face the potbellied man. "That's too steep. Half is enough. Give her back fifty."

The two men regarded one another for a long moment; then Orley turned and slowly moved into the room toward the bar. A safe was there, and he knelt behind the bar to open it.

"Bring us a bottle, too," Pony said.

Matt Bledsoe said in a low voice, "The bastard plays both ends against the middle. My money says he sent those bounty hunters to the Roost."

Cole nodded. Presently Joe Orley returned and handed Molly some wadded greenbacks. She put them in her handbag without counting them.

After bringing a bottle of bourbon and four glasses, Orley left the room to scramble a dozen eggs and fry ham. Molly sat with them at the table, and she drank the amber liquor that Cole poured for her.

Cole drank, then said, "You're right about Orley, Matt. I can feel it in my bones."

"He needs a lesson," Pony said.

"That he does," Matt said. "A painful one."

Cole shook his head. "We've seen enough trouble for a while." He tipped the glass to his lips and emptied it. "I don't think I'll ride this way again. The Roost has always been a miserable place. Now, it isn't even safe. Too many jokers like Orley who'll sell their mothers to collect a piece of the U.P. reward."

Matt nodded agreement. "I'd sooner take my chances somewhere else—Hole-in-the-Wall, maybe."

"Or Star Valley," Pony said.

"Or Brown's Hole," Cole said. "We can shoot deer there, or catch trout out of the Snake."

Molly listened while the three of them reminisced about times they had spent in various hideouts along the Outlaw Trail. None of these places were unknown to lawmen, but they were all fortified and lonely. In the past, few lawmen or bounty hunters would venture into them, but now that the Union Pacific had raised the ante, perhaps the rules of the game had changed. This discussion ended when Joe Orley returned with plates of steaming food.

After the late-night meal, Molly was shown by Orley to the same room she'd occupied before. This time she slid the bunk against the door and went to sleep with her Colt .38 in hand.

She was awakened by a light tapping on the door and opened her eyes to cool darkness. She sat up. The tapping started again. She leaned toward the door, raising her revolver as she drew back the hammer. The mechanism made a well-oiled *click*.

"Who is it?"

The tapping stopped. "Cole."

Molly let the hammer down and got out of bed. She pulled the bunk aside and opened the door. From the dim light in the hall, she saw that he was fully dressed, with his hat pushed back on his head and his gunbelt slung over one shoulder.

"I wanted to see you before we rode out," he said in a low voice.

"You're going now?" she whispered.

"Soon," Cole replied. "Too risky to stay here."

Molly stepped aside. "Come in."

She closed the door behind him, then moved around the bunk and sat on it, pulling the blanket around her. In the dark room, she sensed his presence more than saw him. He came near, and she caught the scent of his manly odor.

"Sit here," Molly said. She felt the bunk sway when he sat down on it, and she heard his gunbelt drop to the plank floor. She felt him watching her in the near-darkness.

"You knew those bounty hunters had been here, didn't you?" Cole asked.

Molly could not see the expression on his face as he spoke. "I told you I'd seen them here. I didn't know who they were. I thought they were fugitives."

"Orley was friendly with them?" Cole asked.

Molly paused. "As friendly as he is to anyone." In the darkness she heard a rattle of paper. She sensed that Cole had not come here just to question her about the bounty hunters.

"I wrote a message to the kid," Cole said. "Will you take it to him?"

"Of course," Molly said. She reached out, and in the darkness her hand met Cole's. He gave her an envelope, and for a moment rested his hand on hers.

"I reckon I ought to see him," Cole said, "but right now I can't. The U.P.'s making things too hot for me."

"I understand," Molly said.

Cole said, "Seems like a lot of things have changed since you came into my life."

Molly was not certain how he meant that until she became aware of his breath on her face. His lips touched her nose, then found her mouth. He kissed her long and gently, and ran a hand through her hair to the back of her neck.

Molly felt the growing flame of passion deep within her, and she returned his kiss, grasping him. Cole moved his hands down her neck to her shoulders and downward. She pulled away, and he caressed her, murmuring with his own rising excitement. He reached down to her legs and pushed her nightgown up to her thighs.

Wonderfully aroused now, Molly raised up and pulled the nightgown above her hips and over her head. She gave her hair a shake and reached out in the darkness, touching his shirt. She found the top button and undid it.

"Take your clothes off," she said.

Afterward they lay together in her bunk, moist from their mingling perspirations. Molly breathed deeply and sighed.

"You're a lot of woman," Cole said. "You make a man think new thoughts."

She turned on her side, pressing her full breasts against his shoulder. "What new thoughts?"

He paused a long while before answering. "After what happened out there in the Roost, I was thinking, this is the worst, lowest, bloodiest life a man can drag himself into. Now I'm thinking that with a woman like you, I could have a different life."

"I thought you didn't want a different life," Molly said.

"I do and I don't," he said. "Sometimes I think I'm getting too old for all this damn running. The thrill isn't what it used to be." He fell silent, then sat up, swinging his legs over the edge of the bunk. "But right now I don't have much choice. Matt and Pony and I have to put some distance between us and this place. The longer we stay here, the longer Joe Orley has to figure out a way to collect a piece of that U.P. reward."

Molly lay on the bunk while Cole dressed. He pulled on his boots and stood, a shadow in the near-darkness. She sensed that he was looking down at her.

"You'll give that message to the kid?" he asked.

"Yes," Molly said.

Cole remained standing over her for a time, then said, "So long," and left the room.

CHAPTER XIV

By the time Molly got up in the morning, Cole Estes and his two partners were long gone. In talking to Joe Orley over a breakfast of cooked oats and oily coffee, she realized he was surprised by the outlaws' quiet departure.

Later in the morning, Molly boarded the north-bound stage. She rode in the rocking coach to Green-river and on to Vernal, Utah. The next day she went on to Rock Springs, Wyoming. On her way to the train depot to buy a ticket to Cheyenne, she was hailed by Marshal Sam Darnell.

"Didn't know if I'd ever see you again or not, Miss Owens," he said, taking off his hat as he approached.

Molly smiled. "I'm hard to kill off."

"Then you made it into the Roost?" Darnell asked.

Molly nodded.

Darnell studied her. "Well, what happened? Did you locate Cole Estes?"

"I accomplished what I set out to do," Molly replied.

Darnell grinned at her vague answer. "Don't worry, Miss Owens, I'm not going to lock you up for associat-ing with a known outlaw—as much as Will Parlow would like me to."

"Will Parlow," Molly said. "Who's he?"

"A former lawman out of New Mexico," Darnell said. "He's hired on with the U.P. He's gathered a posse of half a dozen hardcases, armed them, and mounted them on fast horses. Parlow claims he'll run the Estes gang down, and along the way he'll jail anyone who helps those outlaws."

"Will he do it?" Molly asked.

"He'll sure try," Darnell said. "Parlow is a hard-nosed lawman, Miss Owens, and I hear the U.P. is paying him plenty to get the job done."

Molly went on to the train station. She bought a ticket from the uniformed agent on the next east-bound, due to arrive in three hours. She sat on a bench on the loading platform, thinking of Cole Estes and then of Buck. The message Cole had written was in her handbag in a sealed envelope.

Molly did not realize she had dozed until the distant wail of a train whistle awakened her. She stood and looked down the tracks, seeing a black cloud billowing over the approaching steam engine. From here the engine looked like a dark insect with a single eye, moving down the shining rails.

That enormous wheeled insect emitted bursts of steam when the whistle sounded again, slowed as it rolled past, and drew to a halt. Molly saw the conductor step down from a passenger coach, and he helped several ladies and children climb down the three steps to the loading platform.

Behind them came half a dozen men carrying Winchesters. They were a hard-bitten lot, led by a broad-shouldered, dark-haired man with a grating voice that carried over the sounds of the engine and the other passengers. Molly watched this man order the six men to move down the length of the train to the stock cars.

She climbed aboard and took a window seat, and a few minutes later she saw the armed men leading horses away from the train toward the center of Rock Springs. The horses were sleek and spirited, and even though the animals were safely away from the train when the steam engine's whistle sounded again, they shied and strained against the reins held tautly in the hands of the men who led them.

The train departed, and soon the town disappeared from view. The conductor came through and punched tickets. For a time, Molly looked out at the bleak landscape, then leaned back against the chair and closed her eyes.

She opened them minutes later when the train abruptly slowed and came to a halt. Other passengers in the coach nervously whispered to one another and looked about. Two men in the front, a drummer and a cowhand, drew handguns.

Molly heard snatches of hushed comments while she looked out the window for a clue to what was happening.

". . . robbery, I figure."

". . . trouble on the tracks ahead."

". . . derailed . . ."

The conductor came through the coach. "It's all right, folks, nothing to worry about, just a little delay while we get a problem cleared up." He paused at the front of the passenger coach and asked the two men there to holster their guns.

The door to the rear entrance of the coach swung open, and a man swept in, spurs ringing. Molly turned in the seat and saw that he was the leader of the armed men she'd seen climb off the train in Rock Springs. He had made a hard ride to catch the train.

Looking at each female passenger, he passed Molly, then turned back and stared at her. "Miss Owens?"

"Yes," she said.

"I'd like a word with you," he said. "Come with me, please."

Molly hesitated, sensing that his pretense of courtesy was for the benefit of the onlooking passengers. His tone of voice left no room for discussion.

"Who are you?" she asked.

He gave her a hard stare, then pulled aside his vest. Pinned to his shirt was a brass badge. "Will Parlow, detective for the Union Pacific. This way, please."

Molly met his steady gaze. Parlow wore riding trousers with leather inserts on the insides of the thighs and seat. Strapped around his waist was a cartridge belt and a holstered .45 Peacemaker with walnut grips. He wore an unusual hat for the desert country—narrow-brimmed, with a low crown.

"This way," he repeated.

Molly stood and moved into the aisle. She walked to the rear of the coach and stepped through the open door.

"Keep moving," Parlow ordered.

The door to the next car, the baggage coach, stood open, too. Molly stepped over the car couplings and went inside. Parlow came in behind and closed the door.

Molly turned to face him, sliding her hand into her handbag. She grasped her revolver. Now she saw a long white scar running the length of Parlow's square jaw, parting a day's growth of dark beard stubble. The man, possessed of an air of great intensity, came closer, seeming to bear down on her like a predator.

"Tell me about Cole Estes," Parlow said. "I know you were with him in Robbers Roost."

"Who told you that story?" Molly asked, knowing that he had learned of her trip across the desert from Marshal Darnell and was guessing that she'd found the outlaw.

"I'll ask the questions, Miss Owens," Parlow said in a grating voice. "Your job is to give me the right answers. Do that, and you can go on to your destination." He paused. "But if you play hard to get, I'll haul you back to Rock Springs, where you can sweat out the right answers from a jail cell."

"You talk tough," Molly said, meeting his gaze, "but you have no cause to place me under arrest."

"That's up to me to decide," he said. "I have the power of arrest. We can worry about legal niceties later." Leaning closer, he asked, "Did you or did you not meet with Coles Estes?"

Molly did reply immediately. While she stared into Parlow's unblinking eyes, she thought quickly. It was no secret that after the train robbery, the Cole Estes gang had sought refuge in Robbers Roost. Will Parlow must be headed there, and he would almost certainly interview Joe Orley.

"Yes," Molly said, realizing that the trail would lead back to her eventually.

An expression of triumph briefly crossed Parlow's blocky face. "You trailed the gang into that canyon country, didn't you?"

Molly nodded.

He cast an appraising look at her. "For a pretty lady, all dressed up fancy, you've got sand."

"If you have no more questions, Mr. Parlow—" Molly began.

"Now, hold on," he snapped. "The questions are just starting. I want to know how you got into the Roost. I want to know about his camp, how many men he's got, their arms, everything."

"If you're planning to take a posse into Robbers Roost," Molly said, "I can save you the trouble."

"My plans are none of your business," he said.

Molly met his gaze. "Cole Estes rode out of Robbers Roost with Matt Bledsoe and Pony Diehl. I don't know where they went or even which direction they took."

"You'd like me to think that, I reckon," he said.

Molly shrugged. "Ask Joe Orley."

The remark silenced Parlow. Molly went on to give a brief account of the shoot-out in Robbers Roost, the murders of the women and the Billy Truax gang. She told him Pony Diehl had gunned down the attackers.

"Damned bounty hunters," Parlow said in a growling voice. "They get in the way of law enforcement every time."

"That big reward offered by Union Pacific will bring in more of them," Molly said.

Parlow studied her. "Just where do you fit into the picture? I know you're a Fenton operative."

"You must have had a long talk with Marshal Darnell," Molly said.

"Never mind that," he said. "Answer my question."

"I've told you everything I know about Cole Estes,"

Molly said. "No law requires me to reveal who I'm working for."

"If you've aided and abetted known criminals," Parlow said, "I can run you in."

"You'll have to prove that charge," she said.

He smiled faintly. "I make the charge when I arrest you, then I'll get around to proving it."

"Is that what you intend to do?" Molly asked, her grip tightening around the handle of her revolver in her handbag.

He stared at her, then backed away a step. "I'll let you off this time, lady. If you've lied to me, I'll find out and come hunting for you."

"You make a lot of threats, Parlow," Molly said.

"Not threats," he said. "Promises."

Molly moved forward quickly, and pushed past him. The big man was caught off balance and stumbled back before catching himself.

Opening the door of the baggage coach, Molly left without looking back at him.

CHAPTER XV

"How do I know my father wrote this?" Buck demanded.

Molly had told him of meeting Cole Estes in Robbers Roost and had handed the letter to him. Now she saw Buck's mouth quiver and his eyes blink rapidly as he looked up from the sheet of paper in his hand.

"You have my word," Molly said.

Buck gave a quick, angry shake of his head and turned away. Molly glimpsed a shine of tears in his eyes.

"What did your father write to you?" she asked.

"You don't know?" Buck asked.

"The envelope was sealed when he gave it to me," Molly said.

A long moment passed; then Buck thrust the sheet of paper toward her.

Molly took the letter in her hand and read the words scrawled in pencil.

Kid, you do not know me, but I reckon you have heard of me. Some things you read are true, most are not. But why you want to hunt me up, I do not know. No good will come of it, so quit trying.

I have made a life for myself that I would not wish off on anyone. I have lived on the run since I was seventeen, since I fell in love with the girl who became your mother. When I say girl, I mean just that, because she was younger than me by a couple years. And here you are about the same age now.

But all that business is in the past, a story not worth telling. I got off on the wrong foot and have been running crooked ever since, and after I heard your mother died a year or so after you were born, I had no reason to turn back. I sure as hell can't turn back now.

So, kid, the best I can tell you is try to do better than I have. Don't follow me or my ways. Coming from a good family has some advantages, but it does not count for much in the long haul. You have to go out and make a life for yourself whether you have a family or not, and my advice to you is to get on with yours. Get your schooling. Find work that suits you. Find yourself a good woman. Stay on the top side of every horse you ride.

So long,
Cole Estes

"I should have gone with you," Buck said, his voice thick with emotion. "Things would have been different if I'd been there."

Molly looked up from the letter. "Cole Estes is a man who knows his own mind. He'd have told you this."

"Damn him," Buck said, snatching the letter from Molly's hand. He wadded it up and threw it to the floor. "Damn him!" Suddenly he cried.

Molly stepped to him. She put her arms around him and drew him to her. His narrow body was racked with sobs. She held him tightly, and heard him cry, wet sounds that came from deep inside.

Late in the evening Molly described the dilemma to Mrs. Boatwright.

"What that boy needs is a place to call home," the landlady said, "not a foster home or a home for boys, but *home*; a place that's always there, a place where the door is always open to him, where there's always food on the table, where there's someone to greet him and listen to him."

Molly nodded agreement. "Buck has never known a place like that."

"Well, I'm just the woman to give that to him," Mrs. Boatwright said. "We got along fine while you were gone. The boy's a good worker, and he kept his end of the deal with you. But now that you're back, he probably expects to be shipped right back to the Mike Payton Home for Boys."

"We haven't discussed what's to happen next," Molly said.

"But you can sure guess what's going on inside that red head of his," Mrs. Boatwright said. "He's not used to being wanted. I'll go tell him right now that he has a place here if he wants it—for as long as he wants."

"I looked in on him a while ago," Molly said, "and he was asleep."

Mrs. Boatwright paused. "Well, then I'll tell him in the morning—first thing."

Morning was too late, as it turned out. Coming downstairs for breakfast, Molly heard a commotion in the hallway. At the bottom of the stairs she saw Mrs. Boatwright being confronted by Esther Raines. Esther was red-faced with anger.

Mrs. Boatwright turned to Molly as she approached. "Esther had some money stolen from her room sometime last night—"

"I was robbed!" Esther Raines exclaimed to Molly. "Robbed while I slept! My purse was stolen, the silk one!"

"Was anything else taken?" Molly asked. "Any of your jewelry?"

"No, just the purse," she said. "Over a hundred dollars was in it, about a hundred and twenty, I'd say." She added, "One of the maids probably did it. I want you to have them investigated, Mrs. Boatwright."

"I will," Mrs. Boatwright said, "I most certainly will."

Satisfied for the moment, but still huffy, Esther Raines said, "I want a full investigation. Perhaps other tenants were robbed, too."

"There will be a complete investigation, Mrs. Raines," Mrs. Boatwright said. "If someone who works here is a thief, that person will be discharged, and your money will be returned. I promise you that."

Esther Raines turned away and moved down the hall like a ship on the sea. When she turned and mounted the staircase, Mrs. Boatwright spoke to Molly in a low voice. "He's gone."

"Buck?" Molly asked.

Mrs. Boatwright nodded.

Molly went downstairs to Buck's room by the coal furnace. The bed was neatly made, and the room was clean. No clothes were left behind.

As Molly turned away to leave, her eye was caught by a piece of paper behind the bed. Leaning over the bed, she pulled out an envelope that had evidently fallen there and escaped Buck's notice.

Inside she found the crumpled letter Cole had written, along with several newspaper articles. Some were yellowed with age. Molly flipped through them and found them all to be about the exploits of the Cole Estes gang.

Molly stepped outside through the back door of the mansion, wondering which way Buck had gone. She walked across the yard to a trimmed hedge that marked the rear boundary of the property. She moved alongside the hedge until she reached a gap that opened into the back alley. There, on the ground, she saw the silk purse, wet with dew and almost shimmering in the morning light.

"No money inside," Molly said as she handed the damp purse to Mrs. Boatwright, "but I think he left everything else behind."

Mrs. Boatwright looked into the purse briefly, then asked, "Where did he go, Molly?"

"My guess is that he's headed for the Hole-in-the-Wall in Wyoming," Molly said, remembering where he was going the first time she had met him.

"You'll go after him?" she asked.

Molly nodded.

Mrs. Boatwright looked down at the purse thoughtfully. "I'm going to put a hundred and twenty dollars in here and return it to Esther. I'll tell her the thief must have dropped it in the yard." She added, "When you catch up with Buck, tell him that he owes me."

Molly worked quickly. After packing clean clothes and her gear, Mrs. Boatwright's driver took her to Union Station. She bought a ticket to Cheyenne on the afternoon northbound, then described Buck to several porters and asked if they had seen him. One thought he might have seen a red-haired boy Buck's age climb on the morning train to Cheyenne, but was uncertain when Molly questioned him more closely. The morning had been a busy one, filled with travelers coming and going.

The northbound left Denver shortly after noon and arrived in Cheyenne in the evening. Molly found a ticket agent there who remembered Buck. He had sold the boy a ticket on the short rail line that ran to Casper.

"That red-headed kid had to run to make the train," the ticket agent recalled with a grin.

The next train to Casper, Molly learned, did not depart until tomorrow afternoon. A stagecoach left for Casper early in the morning, but with its many stops along the way, would arrive in Casper several hours later than the train.

Molly checked into the Plainsman Hotel, knowing full well that she was losing ground to Buck. He had stumbled onto the right train connections and had covered a great deal of ground today. All Molly could do now was hope that she could make up the difference after she reached Casper. The trail would be colder by then, though, and people might not remember seeing a red-haired boy of fourteen.

These thoughts occupied Molly's mind as she came down the stairs and crossed the lobby to the restaurant. A saloon was adjacent to the hotel restaurant, and as she passed by the batwing doors, a man lurched out and bumped into her.

" 'Scuse me, ma'am," he said, and lurched away.

Molly glanced after him and saw that he wore a long duster of soiled cotton material and a shapeless hat. He reeked of body odor and whiskey.

Molly had gotten a glimpse of the man's face, and she had entered the restaurant and been seated before she remembered where she'd seen him before. That man had been in the U.S. marshal's office in Denver. The clerk there had read aloud the Union Pacific wanted poster on Cole Estes. After the man was gone, the clerk had muttered in disgust, "Bounty hunter."

CHAPTER XVI

Molly watched for the bounty hunter later in the evening when she sat in the lobby of the Plainsman Hotel reading a newspaper. But he did not pass by, and in the morning, she did not see him in town. When she boarded the train to Casper, she half-expected him to be among the passengers.

The train was a freight pulling one passenger coach. Molly boarded and took a seat at the rear of the coach, and when the steam engine gave three blasts of its whistle and rolled out of the depot, she was relieved to see that the bounty hunter was not aboard. Perhaps he had given up the search for Cole Estes, and his presence here in Cheyenne was only a bizarre coincidence.

The train angled north out of Cheyenne. The steel wheels of the cars played their monotonous music on the rails, and the coach rocked back and forth. As Molly looked out the window and saw Cheyenne slide out of her view, she had second thoughts and began to doubt that seeing the bounty hunter here was a coincidence. The man possessed determination, a crude notion of purpose. Molly had sensed that much about him, and believed he was not one to give up the chase.

Unbathed and unkempt, the bounty hunter had looked down-and-out. Most likely he was not on this train because he could not afford a ticket and space for his horse in a stock car.

If that was the case, he was probably headed into the outlaw country of central Wyoming on horseback, possibly leading a packhorse. That would put him a full day behind her, perhaps two.

The reward offered by Union Pacific was certainly accomplishing its purpose, Molly reflected as the train steamed northward, trailing a black cloud of coal smoke that drifted past the coach windows. No telling how many other bounty hunters were on the trail right now, eager to collect. Between bounty hunters and the posse led by Will Parlow, the famous Cole Estes gang would have their hands full. The Hole-in-the-Wall, an outlaw stronghold first used by Civil War deserters, might not be a safer haven than Robbers Roost had turned out to be.

But Cole Estes was a man who could take care of himself. He'd lived on the run off and on for many years and had been pursued by many posses. He and Matt Bledsoe and Pony Diehl had outsmarted and outshot them all.

Buck was another matter. The boy was driven by a single and simple purpose, an overwhelming desire to see his father. He had no idea what he was riding into.

The Hole-in-the-Wall was a hard day's ride from Casper. Upon climbing down from the passenger coach, Molly hired a porter to carry her luggage to the Casper House, then found a livery stable. She picked out a black, deep-chested saddle horse and arranged for the animal to be delivered to the hotel at six in the morning.

A new oil refinery had opened in Casper, and the town of several hundred residents was experiencing something of a boom. That night, Molly lay in a brass bed in her room on the second floor of the Casper House, hearing raucous sounds from the saloon district, tinny music from upright pianos, mixed with occasional shouts and bursts of drunken laughter. Sleep came quickly.

When the knock on her door came at five-thirty in the morning, Molly awoke with the fading image of a dream in her mind. The dream was of her brother, and as she pulled on her riding clothes, she remembered his smiling face.

From morning to early evening Molly rode over sagebrush-covered hills and down into grassy draws of central Wyoming, moving steadily northward into cattle country. Late in the afternoon she cut west, and before sundown drew in sight of the famous red wall.

The color of the sandstone was remarkably similar to the stone cliffs she'd seen in Robbers Roost, but the comparison ended there. This was a single wall stretching for miles south and north, broken in a few narrow gaps.

This natural barrier had turned away many lawmen, from those who had pursued Frank and Jesse James after the Deadwood holdup in 1877 to posses chasing Big Nose George and Dutch Henry in later times. Molly had read that a gap in the red sandstone could be manned by one or two men with rifles, who could hold off an army. This threat alone had turned back many posses over the years.

Her destination was the settlement of Barnum, just inside the wall. As Molly followed the rutted wagon road through this hole in the red wall, she saw clearly that the life of any lawman would be in the hands of a rifleman stationed on top of the cliff.

But this evening, if a guard was up there, he let Molly pass through. The saddle horse tossed his head, and Molly knew she was approaching the settlement.

A quarter of a mile farther, angling down through a stand of cottonwoods, she saw a random collection of log cabins and frame buildings. In the light of evening, they were unpainted rectangles on the edge of a vast field of grass.

The valley behind the wall, high with grass that gently waved in a breeze, was long and wide, backed by rough hills to the west. The middle fork of the Powder River ran through this big valley. Molly was no rancher, but it did not take a seasoned cowman to see that this back country was perfect for grazing cattle.

She rode into the settlement and saw that Barnum was a crossroads for the wagon route she had followed and another rutted road that ran north and south, paralleling the red wall.

Most of the buildings were abandoned. A small general store appeared to be in business, and she noticed that the windows of a few cabins were covered by curtains. Flowers grew along the walk of a large cabin across the street from the general store.

Three ragged, tail-wagging dogs loped out to greet her as she turned toward a weathered barn on the north edge of Barnum. An old sign over the outsized barn door read "Livery."

Molly reined up at the trough by the pole corral. She stiffly swung down from the saddle. While the horse noisily drank, the barn door squealed on its hinges. Molly loosened the cinch and looked over the saddle to see the livery man approach.

Dressed in patched overalls and a straw hat, the old-timer was lame. But he was spry. He picked up a stone and pitched it at one of the dogs that had edged in close behind Molly.

"Git!" the liveryman said. His aim was poor, but the point was made. All three dogs tucked their tails and slunk away.

"Howdy, ma'am," he said, eyeing her. The old man did not conceal his surprise to see a woman traveling alone on horseback.

"My horse needs a nosebag full of oats," Molly said, "and a long rest in a comfortable stall."

The liveryman grinned toothlessly. "Fer fifty cents, I'll see he gets both." His gaze went to the horse's brand. "Ride in from Casper?"

Molly nodded as she handed the reins to him.

"Figured so," he said shrewdly. "H&B Livery runs this brand down in Casper."

"I could use a feedbag and a comfortable stall myself," Molly said.

He cackled in a high-pitched laugh. "Barnum ain't got a real café or *ho*-tel no more, but Miz Andrews down there takes boarders. I reckon she's got an extry bed."

Molly turned and saw that he pointed toward the cabin with flowers growing along the walk. From here she saw a frame addition on the back. Behind it stood three outhouses, a sign of more prosperous times.

"Thanks," Molly said. She untied her saddlebags and valise from behind the cantle and stepped back as the old-timer led the horse away.

"By the way," Molly said after him, "I'm looking for a fourteen-year-old boy. He might have ridden this way. He's thin, with red hair—"

"Yep," he said over his shoulder.

"What?" Molly exclaimed.

"I seen him," the liveryman said, stopping. "Came through this mornin' on a wind-broke horse. That plug was wheezin' like a steam engine. We made us a trade, and he rode out on a spotted mare."

"Which direction?" Molly asked.

"First he rode north, then he came back this afternoon," he said. He added, "Told me he was hunting for the Outlaw Ranch."

Molly waited for him to continue, but he did not. "You gave him directions?"

"Nope."

She waited again, then asked, "Well, where did he go from here?"

"Nowheres," he said, cackling. "That boy's tail was a-dragging. He left the mare here and went down to Miz Andrews' for a meal. Ain't come back. Reckon he found a bed."

Molly turned away and walked hurriedly down the rutted street toward the cabin with the flower-lined walk. He legs were sore from a long day in the saddle, but now she knew the ride had been worth it. Buck had made a wrong turn this morning, and she'd closed the distance.

CHAPTER XVII

The woman known in Barnum as "Miz Andrews" was a wispy, birdlike lady in a plain gingham dress and heavy shoes, gray-haired but of indeterminate age. She was one of those small, compact women, Molly thought as she was shown into the sparsely furnished cabin, who had probably changed very little in the last two decades.

Miz Andrews had told Molly that she did have a room empty and was glad to have "female company." She cast a measuring look at Molly, smoothing her own dress as she did so.

"Is that what the young gals are wearing these days?" Miz Andrews asked.

"This is my riding outfit," Molly explained. "I have a dress packed that is more . . . respectable."

"Oh, I wasn't meaning to criticize," Miz Andrews said quickly, her hands fluttering in front of her like a pair of butterflies taking flight. "I don't get out much, so I lost track of fashions." She went on, "I like your skirt. It looks practical, good for sitting in a real saddle. I've always believed the sidesaddle was invented by a man who hated women."

Molly laughed. "You may be right about that, Miz Andrews."

The log cabin was little more than a homestead structure, a single room furnished with a table and chairs and one rocker, but the frame addition connected by a doorway in the back wall contained half a dozen small sleeping rooms and a bathroom.

Miz Andrews took Molly back there, and spoke in a

low voice. "I'll put you next to the bathroom, and I'll bring hot water. Then we can talk about supper. I only have one other guest, a youngster who's been sleeping since this afternoon. I've got a notion he'll wake up hungry as a young wolf."

"That youngster is the reason I'm here, Miz Andrews," Molly said.

The woman looked at her in great surprise. "Well," she said after a pause, "it's none of my affair, but he did come here asking about the Outlaw Ranch that he'd read about in some newspaper. Has he done something bad?"

"No," Molly said. "He ran away from his home in Denver."

"Oh, I see," she whispered. "And you aim to stop him before he does do something bad," Miz Andrews suggested.

That was close enough to the truth, and Molly replied with a nod.

Fresh bread was out of the oven and beef stew was simmering on the iron stove when Buck came into the room. Seeing Molly at the table with Miz Andrews, a teacup in her hand, he stopped in mid-stride.

"Hello, Buck," Molly said.

The boy blinked, at a loss for words for a full thirty seconds. Dressed in clothes rumpled from sleep, he came to the table. "I wondered if you'd ride after me."

Molly met his gaze until Miz Andrews broke the silence. The slight woman slid her chair back and said she would get supper.

The meal was eaten in silence, amid a few feeble attempts at conversation. After a dessert of apple dumplings, Miz Andrews' left the table and began cleaning dishes.

Buck leaned toward Molly. "I'm going to pay Miss Raines back," he said.

"Mrs. Boatwright already did," Molly said. "You owe her." She went on to explain about the purse, then asked the question that had been on her mind ever since she left Denver. "Is anyone else riding after you?"

"You mean, did I steal anything else?" Buck asked, his voice rising. He quickly lowered his voice when Miz Andrews glanced over her shoulder at him. "No, I paid for everything I needed to get this far—train tickets, two horses, food, everything."

"Where will you go from here?" she asked.

"To the Outlaw Ranch," Buck said, "if I can find the damned place. Nobody around here will tell me where it is." He paused. "But I'll find it. Nobody's going to stop me."

"I'm not trying to stop you," Molly said.

Buck's eyes narrowed with suspicion again. "I don't see any other reason for you to ride after me."

"I want to help," Molly said.

"You can help by telling me where the Outlaw Ranch is," he said.

"I don't know where it is," Molly said. "But there are ways of getting information—"

"I know where it is," Miz Andrews interrupted.

Molly saw the small woman turn away from the pan of soapy water and dry her hands on a dish towel. She came to the table.

"I couldn't help but overhear," Miz Andrews said, looking at Buck. "Just why are you so all-fired eager to join up with outlaws?"

"I'm not," Buck said. "I want to see my father, that's all."

"Who's your pa?" Miz Andrews asked.

"Cole Estes," he replied.

Miz Andrews' mouth opened in surprise. She recovered, and cast a questioning glance at Molly.

"It's true," Molly said. "Is Cole here?"

"Matt Bledsoe rode in the other day," she said, "and bought supplies across the street."

"Bledsoe!" Buck exclaimed. "I've read about him!"

"Can you tell us where the Outlaw Ranch is?" Molly asked.

"Sure, I can," Miz Andrews said. "It isn't a ranch, not a real one. It's a bunch of cabins built together like a fort. Strangers aren't welcome, especially not since the Johnson County War."

"War?" Buck asked. "A war was fought here?"

Miz Andrews nodded. "It's a long story, Buck, but to put it in a nutshell, the big ranchers got to believing they were being robbed blind, so they hired a bunch of gunmen to come up here and kill off our men. They killed Nate Champion, murdered him over at the K.C. Ranch. He was a good man . . ."

Her voice shook with emotion as she continued. "But we whipped them. Our men got those killers surrounded, and every one of them would be six feet under Johnson County soil if the governor hadn't talked President Harrison into sending a company of Negro cavalry to their rescue."

Molly looked at the woman's face while she fought tears. Lines in her face deepened, showing the anguish of remembering. Local men had been killed not far from here, and even three years after the famous "invasion," anger and outrage ran high in Johnson County.

"So that's why there's no sympathy for the cattle barons around here," Miz Andrews went on, "and that's why nobody gives information to strangers."

"But all I want to do is find my father," Buck said.

"I know," she said, "but it's too dangerous for you to ride in there. Some bad apples come through the Hole-in-the-Wall, and one of them might gun you down for pleasure. I don't want that on my conscience."

"A boy and a woman traveling together might not draw gunfire," Molly suggested.

Miz Andrews considered the idea, and nodded. "I reckon so."

"Then you'll tell us?" Buck asked, leaning forward in his chair.

"Tell you what I will do, youngster," Miz Andrews said. "I'll give directions to Molly. That way, you'll have to stick with her, and you won't be running off on your own again."

Unable to conceal his disappointment and anger, Buck scowled and swore under his breath.

"It's for your own good," Miz Andrews insisted. "I overheard enough to know you've got ideas of your own, some of them poor. Make a mistake out here, and you'll pay with your life. You're lucky Molly thinks enough of you to try to keep you alive awhile longer."

Late in the night Molly was awakened by the sounds of horsemen on the street outside. The drumming of hooves came into her sleep, and she awakened to hear men's voices. One voice was deeper than the others, and commanding in tone.

Presently the horsemen rode out, and Molly drifted back into sleep, vaguely aware that the men had roused the storekeeper across the street.

Over breakfast early in the morning, nothing was said about the riders in the night. Buck must have slept through the disturbance, which was just as well. Molly decided Miz Andrews either had not heard the men or she knew who they were and was protecting them by not discussing their presence.

After the breakfast of eggs and sausage and hot buttered muffins with honey, Miz Andrews gave Molly a lingering glance. Buck had gone to fetch their saddlebags.

"You be careful, now," the woman said.

Chapter XVIII

Molly and Buck rode south, parallel to the red wall. With the sun rising to their left, they followed the narrow road over low hills covered with grass, a road that was deeply rutted by the iron-tired wheels of wagons.

The day was beautiful. Cottony clouds were fluffed high in the blue sky, and a cooling morning breeze rippled across the high grass. This fine pastureland, still unfenced, was part of the Bar C Ranch. The Bar C was a working cattle ranch, Molly had been told by Miz Andrews, and the cattle bearing that brand were left alone by all the real rustlers and accused rustlers who sought refuge here.

Late in the morning, Molly topped a rise that overlooked Bar C headquarters, and she signaled Buck to halt. In the coulee below were several log buildings amid tall cottonwood trees and a pond. Ducks swam on the pond, and on the grassy bank were several geese and goslings.

"Peaceful scene, isn't it?" Molly asked.

Buck nodded as he looked down at the ranch buildings. "Someday I'll own a place like that."

Molly smiled at him. This was the first time she'd ever heard him make a wish for the future.

Molly turned off the road here and led the way along the top of the hill, skirting the ranch. A mile beyond, she dropped down the sloping side of the grassy hill. Grazing in a wide valley here were several hundred cattle, well-fed and sleek.

They rode around the Bar C herd, and following

Miz Andrews' directions, Molly headed for the high rock-crowned hills on the horizon to the west. Before noon she and Buck came in sight of a group of log cabins.

Molly dropped back, urgently motioning for Buck to follow. Behind a swell of ground she dismounted and took out her field glasses from the leather case hanging from the saddle horn.

Molly walked upslope toward the crest and dropped to her knees in the grass. Buck came behind. He followed her example and crawled with her to the top.

The sweet smell of grass filled her nostrils as she brought the field glasses to her eyes and focused the lenses. Buck stretched out beside her, breathing sharply with excitement.

"There it is!" he whispered.

He was right. Molly saw that the compound of log cabins had been accurately described by Miz Andrews. There were six, all small and stout. Open ground stretched out on all sides. An approaching rider could be seen from a great distance, giving the inhabitants ample time to decide whether a friend or enemy was coming.

"Let me look," Buck said.

Molly handed the field glasses to him. So intent was their concentration on the cabins that neither heard the footfalls on the slope behind them.

"What the hell are you doing here?"

Molly whirled around. Standing half a dozen paces away was Will Parlow, hands on his hips. Behind him were three men in the Union Pacific posse. They were well-dressed and armed with new Winchester repeating rifles and Peacemaker revolvers holstered on cartridge belts.

"Mr. Parlow," Molly said in greeting. She got to her feet, now realizing that deep, commanding voice she'd heard in Barnum last night belonged to him, and the drumming hoofbeats of the night riders had been his posse.

Buck sat up in shocked silence, wide-eyed, and the field glasses dropped to the grass.

"We're touring the Wyoming countryside," Molly said. "Lovely day, isn't it?"

Parlow scowled. "Another smart answer like that will get you a pair of leg irons." He paused. "You're hooked up with Cole Estes somehow. That's plain." He glanced at Buck, then said to Molly, "Tell me your story, Miss Owens, and tell it straight. You won't get a second chance."

"And I won't be threatened by you," Molly said. "Now, I suggest you go about your business and leave us alone."

Parlow stared at her, then jerked his head at his men. "Take them."

Molly watched as Parlow folded his arms over his chest and the three men came forward, rifles at the ready. They looked sheepish and determined at once. The idea of capturing a woman and a boy was not one they had considered until now.

Under different circumstances, Molly might have resisted. The element of surprise would have been on her side if she had drawn her revolver and aimed it point-blank at Parlow a moment ago. But she could not take any action that would endanger Buck. The boy slowly stood, picking up the field glasses. He cast a fearful look at Molly. She gave him a brief smile, hoping to assure him that everything would be all right.

"Hold it!" Parlow said suddenly. "Keep her covered. These damned Fenton operatives carry sneak guns."

Molly stood still as Parlow moved to her. She felt his heavy hands on her waist and hips; then he moved up to her chest. He grasped her breasts.

"Make you feel good?" Molly asked.

Parlow grinned.

"Damn you!" Buck shouted. "Get your goddamned hands off her!" He lunged at Parlow, swinging the field glasses at his head.

But before the boy reached his target, one of the deputies thrust his rifle barrel out. The end of it punched into Buck's ribs, sending him off balance. Buck rolled to the ground.

Briefly shaken, Parlow had backed away. Now he came forward, while the three deputies gathered around the boy.

"You lousy bastards!" Buck shouted.

"Shut that mouth of yours," Parlow said, "or we'll gag you." He looked at Molly, then pulled her jacket aside. With a triumphant grunt he yanked the Colt Lightning-model revolver from her shoulder holster. "All right," he said, backing away. "March them back to camp."

Buck scrambled to his feet and followed Molly's example by walking silently in front of the deputies. One of them brought their horses.

The coulee deepened. Rounding a bend 150 yards away, Molly saw a rope corral. Saddle horses were inside. The men of the Union Pacific posse, a larger force than Molly had seen in Rock Springs, lounged in the grass nearby. A dozen men were here. One sat near the top of the rise, from where the Outlaw Ranch could be observed in the distance. That man must have seen Molly and Buck ride in from the Bar C Ranch.

"Over there," Parlow ordered, pointing to the high grass beyond the rope corral.

Molly walked around the horses. Buck moved closer to her.

"I'm going to kill these bastards," he whispered. "Every damned one of them."

Molly put her hand on the boy's shoulder. "For now we'll go along and do what we're told."

"For now," Buck said grimly.

Parlow ordered them to sit in the grass. He reached into his hip pocket and drew out a pair of handcuffs. "Stick out your right hand, lady. You, boy, pull off your left boot."

Molly did as he ordered, and felt steel encircle her wrist, fastened snugly in a cool bracelet.

"Hurry it up, boy," Parlow said in a growling voice.

Molly watched Buck take off his boot, noted that he wore no sock, and then was yanked forward as Parlow pulled the handcuff toward him and snapped it around Buck's bony ankle.

"That ought to slow you down," Parlow said with a short laugh.

Molly looked up at him. "We were in your way?"

"Damned right, you were," he said.

"What's your plan?" Molly asked. "Attack the Outlaw Ranch tonight?"

Parlow scowled. "That's none of your damned business, Fenton lady." He added, "After we get our work done here, I'm going to find out exactly what your connection with Cole Estes is. If you're in with him, I'll bring you before a judge who'll jail you and throw the key away." He turned and strode through the grass. Molly watched him climb the slope, where he joined the guard.

Buck sat up, leaning against Molly. "Who are these men?" he whispered urgently.

Molly quietly explained that they were a special posse working for the Union Pacific Railroad, a dozen professional gunmen hunting robbers of U.P. express coaches. She did not mention that Parlow wanted above all else to bring in Cole Estes, dead or alive.

The afternoon dragged toward sundown as Molly and Buck alternately lay back in the grass together or sat up, watching the men. Molly was impressed by Parlow's command of the men and his strict leadership. The gunmen waited like soldiers before a battle, talking quietly among themselves or resting. None smoked. They ate cold beef and bread, washed down with water from canteens.

At sundown the men stirred. They got to their feet and checked their guns. One took down the rope corral, and the others caught their horses and saddled them. Parlow came down from the crest of the rise, followed by the guard.

"Good breeze now," Parlow said quietly. "Let's move out."

Molly did not understand his plan until she saw that several of the riders held oil-soaked torches. She watched them ride farther down the coulee, disappearing around a bend.

Molly raised up to all fours. "Stand up and walk to my horse."

"We can't ride like this!" Buck said in surprise.

"Do as I tell you," Molly said, tugging at the handcuffs that bound her wrist to his ankle. "Come on!"

They moved awkwardly at first, with Buck taking short steps while Molly crawled. But soon they made good progress.

The saddle horse perked his ears, then rolled his eyes and shied away from this strange sight. Molly spoke in a low, soothing voice. The horse pranced away a few steps and tossed his head. Molly spoke again and at last calmed the animal. She edged close enough for Buck to reach out and grab the reins.

"Get my handbag," Molly said.

Holding the reins in one hand, Buck reached back with his other hand and untied the handbag behind the cantle. He handed it down to her.

Molly opened the top flap of the handbag and reached into it. She brought out a small leather case. Inside was a set of lock probes.

Aware that Buck watched in silent fascination, she tried one probe in the lock, then another. Turning it slowly, she felt for the release. On the third try, the steel bracelets snapped open.

"How did you do that?" Buck asked in amazement.

Molly stood, rubbing her wrist. She saw that one of the U.P. posse had looped her field glasses over the saddle horn. Snatching them off the saddle horn, she sprinted up the side of the coulee. Near the crest she dropped down and crawled up until she saw the cabins in the distance.

Buck had gone back for his boot. By the time he pulled it on and came up the slope where he flopped down beside Molly, Parlow's plan had already been put into action. White smoke drifted into the air along a line upwind from the Outlaw Ranch.

Molly focused the field glasses. She saw a growing sheet of flame below the billowing smoke. The steady breeze would carry the fire to the compound of cabins in a matter of minutes. Downwind, Parlow and his gunmen waited.

CHAPTER XIX

In range country, few catastrophes were dreaded more than a grass fire. Now Molly saw why, and as she looked at the flames racing toward the compound of cabins, she saw that it made a fearsome weapon.

In the distance Molly heard shouts as men ran out of the cabins toward the pole corral. Molly knew that cowhands would stand and fight a range fire, but Parlow must have been betting these men were outlaws who would flee. He was right.

The flames ignited the cabins of the Outlaw Ranch, and leaped up the sides of the log walls. The inhabitants, made small by distance, hurriedly saddled their horses. The animals were frightened by the scent of smoke and the sounds of crackling flames, and inside the corral they milled and bucked while the men tried to control them.

Several men rode out of the compound, galloping away from the flames, and rode straight at Parlow's men. The riders were cut down by a single volley of rifle fire. They spilled out of their saddles, and the horses veered away at full gallop.

The half-dozen men remaining at the cabins now were warned of the ambush, but seemed unable to avoid it. Molly saw them mounted near the cabins, bunched together, waving their arms. Then they spurred their prancing horses and rode out to open ground, cutting an angle between the flames in the grass and the hidden riflemen.

The dash was ill-fated. A volley of rifle fire, followed by sporadic shooting from Parlow's men, dropped all the men and wounded several horses. The men lay still, and the flames swept over them.

Buck sobbed, burying his face in his arms. Molly lowered the field glasses and put her arm around him, pulling his narrow shoulders to her.

"Go back to the horses, Buck," she said softly. "Wait for me there."

Buck nodded and wiped the back of a hand over his eyes. Raising up, he turned and got to his feet, head bowed.

Molly watched him walk down the slope to their horses; then she turned and brought the field glasses to her eyes.

The land, formerly waving with high grass, now was charred, and the log cabins were in flames. A smear of smoke darkened the sky over them. Swinging the glasses to her right, Molly saw blackened lumps on the ground that were the remains of the men who had fled the fire. Beyond them, Molly caught a glimpse of movement.

Through the screen of smoke drifting up from the smoldering grass, Molly saw horsebackers. The smoky haze made them ghostly, a dozen grim reapers with rifles at the ready, coming in a line across the blackened land toward the charred bodies.

She did not have to linger to know what would happen next. Parlow and his riders would try to identify the remains, and they would search the ruins of the Outlaw Ranch. Then Will Parlow would come back here.

Molly pushed to her feet and quickly walked down the slope toward the horses. Passing Buck, she went to her horse. She shoved the field glasses into the case and looked back when she heard Buck. He was sobbing.

"We have to ride out of here," Molly said, tossing the strap of the field-glasses case over her saddle horn.

Buck cast an angry, defiant look at her. "I'm not

leaving. I'm going to kill that Parlow bastard . . .
shoot him down . . . just like he shot down my father."

"Buck," Molly said, "your father may not have
been there."

"What?" he asked.

"From that distance, I couldn't see faces," Molly
said, "but I didn't see anyone who looked like him—
or Pony Diehl or Matt Bledsoe."

Buck stared at her openmouthed, as though he
could not grasp the meaning of her words.

"Mount up," Molly said, stepping into the saddle.
"The first thing we have to do is put some distance
between us and Parlow. Then we'll hunt for Robbers
Cave."

Buck blinked. "Robbers Cave?"

Molly gestured to hills on the western horizon.
"Miz Andrews told me about an old outlaw hideout in
those hills. If Cole Estes is in this country, we'll
probably find him in that cave." She paused. "Or we
can ride back for Denver."

"No!" Buck exclaimed. He went to his mare. "Let's
ride."

Molly led the way, following the winding southward course of a ravine that concealed them from
view. Three miles away from the site of Parlow's
camp, the land flattened out. In open ground now,
Molly and Buck spurred their horses straight west
toward the rock-crowned hills.

Molly kept a watchful eye on their back trail. When
they stopped to rest the horses, she pulled out her
field glasses and searched the terrain. She saw no
movement, no dust clouds drifting into the afternoon
sky that would mean Parlow and his posse had picked
up their trail and were pursuing.

By the time Molly and Buck reached the rough
hills, they were squinting into the setting sun. These
hills were steep-sided and covered with loose, flat
stones the size of teacup saucers. This made for slow
going, and the horses picked their way upslope, occa-

sionally sliding back. The ride to the top was tense with the constant danger of the horses losing their footing and falling all the way to the bottom.

An hour later, they made it. The top of the hill was flat sandstone. Few trees grew here. Molly reined up and looked back through the field glasses. The elevation gave her a long view.

"See anything?" Buck asked.

Molly saw no riders, but she did see the blackened field on the flat expanse of ground near the coulee, and she saw the charred remains of the cabins, like a strange skeleton. The fire had burned all the way to the coulee, and to a ravine on the other side, but had stopped there and not burned more pastureland.

Cattle grazed in a field far in the distance. Molly saw no horsebackers. She lowered the field glasses.

"They aren't coming after us," she said. "Parlow must have had all he could handle back there."

Buck swore at the mention of the man's name.

Turning around, Molly tugged down the brim of her Stetson against the setting sun. More hills rumpled the terrain to the west, one after another, like huge folds in an earthen blanket. They were topped with sandstone, and over the centuries the stone had cracked and small pieces had broken away, littering the hillsides.

"Where's Robbers Cave?" Buck asked.

"North of here," Molly said. Miz Andrews had given her general directions, saying it was nearly hidden in the draw below a cliff several miles north and west of here. Molly knew it would be unwise to ride in there tonight.

"Let's ride for it," Buck said.

Molly turned in the saddle and saw his mare standing with her head drooping. "Not this evening, Buck. Right now we have to find water for the horses and a hiding place of our own."

"Hiding place?" Buck asked. "You think Parlow will come after us?"

"I'm not going to make it easy for him if he does," Molly said.

Down in the ravine between this hill and the next one, Molly discovered deer tracks in the soft soil. Following them half a mile to the north, she found a spring. Beyond it, ringed by brush, was a patch of grass, and there they made camp.

The night passed with only the sounds of coyote calls and owl hoots in the distance. All of the morning and much of the next afternoon were spent in a methodical search of the draw beyond the next hill. They ranged far to the north, looking for signs of horses as well as a cave in the sandstone hillside. The vegetation thickened, choking the draw, and made ideal camouflage.

Molly looked back and saw Buck's haggard face. He was tired, but he had lost none of his determination. He studied the ground in his search for signs of horses, and made no complaint.

Through the day they saw deer tracks, and they flushed cottontail rabbits from hiding places in the brush, but they cut no horse trails. Moving north and west, deeper into the rugged hills, they steadily approached a larger, flat-topped hill. Marked by a massive sandstone ledge at the crest, a long, sheer cliff dropped down to vegetation that choked the draw below.

Molly topped the hill overlooking this draw and rode to the edge. She scanned the base of the cliff and then looked straight down, where a flicker of movement caught her eye. Down there in the bottom was a brush corral, well concealed. Half a dozen horses were penned inside.

Buck drew even with her. She glanced at him, seeing a quizzical expression on his face.

"Down there," she said in a low voice.

Buck stood in his stirrups and leaned over, looking down into the bottom of the narrow draw.

"Damn!" he whispered.

"Howdy, Miss Owens."

Molly whirled around in the saddle and looked back. Standing twenty yards away with a double-barreled shotgun in his hands was Matt Bledsoe.

CHAPTER XX

"Fancy meeting you here, lady," Matt Bledsoe said, shifting the shotgun in his hands. He raised the weapon over his head and waved it, sending a signal across the draw toward the high sandstone ledge on the hilltop.

"Pony's had you two in his sights for a quarter of an hour," Bledsoe said. "You're lucky to be alive, mighty lucky." His gaze went from Molly to Buck, and back again. "Who's the boy?"

"Goes by the name of Buck," Molly said. "He wants to talk to Cole—"

"What the hell is this about?" Bledsoe asked impatiently. "Why are you trailing us?"

"I think you know," Molly said, glancing at Buck.

Bledsoe's jaw tightened while he glared at Molly. "Cole told me and Pony we'd seen the last of you. Now you show up again, and trouble is likely right behind you."

"I'm not the one who's causing you trouble," Molly said.

Bledsoe continued glaring at her. At last he said, "All right, get down. Lead your horses this way."

Molly and Buck dismounted and took their horses' reins as they followed Bledsoe along the top of the hill. Less than a hundred yards away he dropped down the side to a faint trail angling downslope. The trail led to the brush corral.

Molly saw now that a small stream ran through the horse pen, making it an ideal reserve for horses.

Bledsoe pulled aside several clumps of dried brush. A wire gate was hidden there.

Bledsoe opened the gate and stepped aside while Molly and Buck led their horses inside. After stripping their saddles and bridles, they came out with saddlebags slung over their shoulders. Bledsoe closed the gate and concealed it with brush.

"This way," Bledsoe said, leading them along the dim trail through the brush. "Walk single file so you don't bust out a bigger path."

The trail led through the bottom of the draw along the stream, crossed over, and angled up the side of the larger hill. Forty yards up, Molly saw a break in the brush. A cave was there. The wide opening was partly covered by a cowhide hanging from above.

Molly glanced over her shoulder. Buck had seen it, too, and now a tense expression lined his face.

"Cole," Bledsoe called as he approached the mouth of the cave. "Cole."

Moments later the cowhide was pulled aside. Cole Estes ducked out, blinking against the light as he straightened up. He was hatless, and his reddish hair was rumpled. He looked at Molly in great surprise; then his gaze cut to Buck.

Buck said in a voice clogged with emotion, "You're my father."

"Cole," Molly said, "this is Oliver James Estes."

A man rarely at a loss for words, Cole was struck silent now. He stood still, rooted at the mouth of the cave under the towering sandstone ledge, and stared at Buck.

The silence was broken when Bledsoe stepped forward and asked, "That right, Cole?" He turned and studied Buck's face. "By God, I do see a resemblance. This your boy, Cole?"

Cole came to Buck, holding out his hand to shake. "I'm proud to meet you . . . Oliver."

"Call me Buck," he said, grasping Cole's hand. "That's the name I answer to."

Cole grinned. "Buck. I like that." He glanced at Molly.

"My being here isn't her fault," Buck said. "She gave me the letter you wrote and told me I should let it go at that. Maybe I should have. But I couldn't, I just couldn't." He wiped a hand across his eyes. "I came to Barnum on my own. Molly rode after me."

Cole nodded that he understood. "You know, I'm glad you came. Ever since Molly told me about you, I've been thinking about you, wondering about you. We need to have a long talk, don't we?"

"Yeah," Buck said, smiling, "we sure do."

Cole motioned to the cowhide covering the cave entrance. "Come in, and we'll do that."

Matt Bledsoe moved away. "I'll check their back trail," he said over his shoulder. He cast a hard glance at Molly.

Cole pulled the cowhide aside. Molly watched Buck duck and step into the cave. Cole motioned her to come in.

Molly shook her head. "This is between the two of you."

"No, I want you to hear this, Molly," he said. "Please."

Molly met his steady gaze, then moved toward him. He put his hand on her shoulder as she bent down and entered the cave.

An oil lamp burned on an upturned crate. By its light, Molly saw three cots heaped with clothes and blankets, and near the back of the cave were boxes containing tins of food.

Cole dumped clothes off one of the cots and pulled it close to another. He motioned for Molly and Buck to sit on them; then he turned an empty wooden box on its end and sat on it.

"Buck, I never was a father to you, and like I wrote to you in that letter, it's a little late for me to start. I don't aim to try." Cole paused, looking at Buck. "Truth is, I never figured you'd feel anything toward me. I was mighty surprised to learn otherwise when Molly caught up with me at the Roost."

"I've always wondered about you," Buck said. "In the orphanage I used to dream about you." He added, "I beat up a kid once for calling me a bastard, beat him good."

Molly saw Cole flinch.

"Well, I'm no prize as a father," Cole said. "The bald truth of the matter is, I never gave much thought to that baby I never saw back in Missouri. I never thought about the baby growing up to be . . . you."

"What happened between you and my ma?" Buck asked. "I know her name was Jennifer, but who was she?"

"A beautiful young woman," Cole replied. "Small and slender, and as light on her feet as a running doe. Folks said we were smitten with puppy love, but we both knew it was something different than that, something better. We were in love, Buck, all the way."

"What happened?" he asked again.

Cole took a deep breath before he answered. "Hard to put everything into words, Buck. I had strong feelings those days, and I was wronged, and then I felt like I ruined Jenny's life. Everything went bad, and I was hiding out when I heard she'd died during childbirth."

Molly heard the words tumble from Cole's mouth, barely understanding the sense of what he said, and realizing he'd never tried to tell this to anyone before.

"You were hiding out?" Buck asked.

Cole nodded. "I worked for a man named Maxfield. I broke horses for him, and when it came time to collect my pay, he put me off. Made some excuse and told me to come back next week. Well, about the second time that happened, I saw his game.

"I went after him with blood in my eye. I knew Jenny was pregnant, and I needed some money so we could get married. Maxfield was a grown man, strong as an ox, and he handed me a whipping. I came back that night and dropped him with a piece of stove wood, bashed his head in proper. I searched his pockets and his whole house and found about fifty dollars, less than half what he owed me.

"I gave the money to Jenny, but I ran off when I heard Maxfield was hurt bad. He wasn't dying, but folks were saying he'd never be the same again. Brains scrambled, or something. I went west, crossed the state line, and went to work in a livery. I'd heard there was a price on my head, but I figured I'd save up some money and go get Jenny one day. Well, months passed, and then I heard she died in childbirth. Guess I went a little loco. I got in a fight and ended up in a jail cell. The sheriff there found out I was wanted back in Missouri. He was fixing to send me back, when I escaped. Been on the run ever since."

Molly watched as father and son looked at one another. She heard Cole say in a low voice, "Don't you make the same mistake, boy."

"But you could have changed," Buck said.

"Back then I could have," Cole said almost wistfully. "I didn't see it that way when I was sixteen, seventeen years old. I was mad at everybody, and I set out to be the best holdup man on two legs. When I hooked up with Matt and Pony, we took on the railroads. Oh, we had some good years, make no mistake. Time was, we could knock over an express coach or a bank, lay low for a few weeks, then come out and spend the loot. Lived high, we did." He looked around at the walls of the cave. "Not anymore."

"But you can still change," Buck insisted.

Cole shook his head. "Not now. I'm in too deep."

CHAPTER XXI

"What does that kid think of me, Molly?"

By starlight she looked at the angular profile of Cole's face. They sat together on a blanket spread on top of the sandstone ledge high above the cave. This was the lookout, and from here Pony Diehl had spotted Molly and Buck riding in from the Hole-in-the-Wall country. Cole had come up here to take his turn at guard duty, and Molly had come with him. The others were in the cave, asleep. Molly had told him what the Union Pacific posse had done at the Outlaw Ranch, and after discussing Will Parlow, darkness closed in, and their talk turned to the boy.

"I'd say he worships the ground you walk on, Cole," Molly replied.

He cut a sharp glance at her. "The hell," he said. After looking out at the hills lighted by stars, he said, "He sure was quiet during supper and after."

"You gave Buck a lot to think about," Molly said.

Cole turned to her again. "You're the one who's given me a lot to think about, Molly Owens."

Molly reached out and touched his face with her fingertips, feeling his smooth, freshly shaven jaw. "The night is warm," she whispered.

Cole kissed her and took her into his arms. Molly returned the kiss, feeling his lips press against hers. Her passion quickly mounting, she held him tightly as they sank back on the blanket, their lips never parting.

Molly ran her fingers over his broad shoulders, drawing her hand up to the back of his neck. She massaged him. He moaned, at last drawing his lips back from hers.

"You're a lot of woman," he said in a low voice.

Molly smiled and unbuttoned his shirt. Reaching in, she ran her hand over his muscular chest. Cole placed his hand on her hip. Molly kissed him again, long and hard.

They undressed in the starlight that shone from the black sky. Far in the distance a coyote yelped, and as Molly dropped her riding skirt at her feet, another answered.

"We have an audience," Cole said.

Molly laughed and stepped into his arms.

Molly looked into the night sky, feeling a new sense of time and space, a larger one than she had ever known.

Cole lay warmly on top of her for a time, then pulled away and stretched out on the blanket beside her. "We silenced those coyotes," he said.

Molly laughed softly and turned to him. She laid her arm over his gently heaving chest and saw him staring up at the sky.

"What's going to become of us?" Cole asked. A long moment passed, and he added, "I mean, all of us—that boy, you, me . . ." His voice trailed off.

"I've never seen into the future," Molly said, noting that Cole did not mention Matt Bledsoe and Pony Diehl.

"Maybe that's what jabs into me," Cole said, turning his head to look at her. "I look at that boy, those eyes of his, and I think about the past, but I'm seeing into the future."

In the morning Molly listened while Cole and Matt Bledsoe discussed the Union Pacific posse. Buck looked on too, eating the last of the cold ham he was having for breakfast. Pony Diehl was standing guard on the hilltop.

"A bunch of killers," Bledsoe said, "that's who

Parlow's got working for him. They're no better than damned bounty hunters."

Yesterday Bledsoe had ridden through the hills to a point overlooking the Hole-in-the-Wall. From a distance he'd seen the smoldering remains of the Outlaw Ranch and the burned field.

"They're killers, all right," Buck said, swallowing a piece of ham. "Molly and I saw them. We were taken prisoner by Parlow." He went on to explain what had happened yesterday.

Bledsoe cast a sidelong glance at Molly. "I told you trouble follows her, Cole."

"I didn't lead anyone to your camp yesterday," Molly said to Bledsoe. "And I'm leaving today."

Both Cole and Buck looked at her in surprise. Cole said, "I want you to stay—both of you."

Molly shook her head.

Cole began to protest.

"There's a time and there's a place for women," Matt Bledsoe interrupted, "and a hideout camp ain't it. You've said that yourself, Cole."

"Matt," Cole said, jerking his head toward the cowhide covering the cave entrance, "go up and spell Pony."

Molly watched the two men regard one another; then Bledsoe stood. He snatched up his shotgun and strode out, whipping the cowhide curtain aside as he left.

"Molly, I want you to stay on another day or two," Cole said. He added, "You and Buck."

"Buck can decide for himself," Molly said, "but I have to get back to Denver. By now my employer's wondering about me."

Cole's gaze lingered on her; then he turned to Buck. "You'd better ride with her, son."

Molly had never heard Cole call him "son," and she turned to see Buck's face twist in anguish. "I want to stay," he said.

Cole shook his head. "Your future is in Denver, not

here in this cave. Ride with Molly, and do what she tells you."

"No—" Buck began.

"Do what I tell you!" Cole snapped. "We're riding out soon. One more big job, and we're heading for South America. Life will be peaceful down there."

Buck looked at him in surprise. "You're leaving the country?"

"That's right," Cole said. "Things are getting too hot around here, and Pony and Matt and I are heading for greener pastures. We'll leave Will Parlow and the rest of the bloodsuckers behind." He paused. "You can't ride with us, son. Get that idea out of your head."

Buck looked downward, staring at his dusty boot tops.

"I'll try to see you again before I leave the United States," Cole said. "Stay in Denver, where I can find you."

Molly studied Buck's expression as the boy looked at his father. She wondered if Buck saw through the lie, and then, as she watched, the boy nodded once.

Cole grinned. "Don't worry. You haven't seen the last of me—neither one of you."

Buck turned in the saddle as his mare labored up the side of the draw overlooking Robbers Cave, never taking his eyes away from the spot where he had last seen his father. At the top of the hill he reined to a halt.

Molly drew up beside him. Across the way she could see neither Matt Bledsoe nor Pony Diehl, but she knew at least one of them was there, watching.

Buck turned to her. "Will we see him again?"

"I don't know," Molly said.

His mouth trembled. "I'm afraid I'll never see my father again."

Molly wanted to offer hope to the boy, but she could not. She doubted Cole Estes would ever risk coming to Denver. He would be a hunted man as long as the big reward was hanging over his head.

Molly turned her horse and rode across the top of the hill. Buck reluctantly followed.

She led the way down the far side, with her horse carefully picking his route on the loose rock. Over the sounds of creaking saddle leather and horseshoes ringing on stone, Molly heard Buck sobbing.

More concerned about the boy than about what lay ahead, Molly rode to the brush-choked bottom without watching for danger ahead. Her horse almost reared when a man leaped out, leveling a large-caliber revolver at her. He wore a soiled duster that reached to his boot tops.

"One damned sound out of either one of you, and you're both dead."

Molly jerked back on the reins and brought her horse under control. She recognized the face under the brim of a dirty hat that had long ago lost its shape. He was the bounty hunter Molly had first seen in Denver and later bumped into in Cheyenne.

CHAPTER XXII

"You Cole Estes' woman?" the bounty hunter demanded.

"I don't know what you're talking about," Molly said, realizing that the man did not recognize her. "We're out for a horseback ride—"

"Shut your lying mouth," he snapped. "This is outlaw country. The cave is just over the hill. I know, because I hid out there myself years ago." He looked at Buck, then back at Molly. "Climb down."

"I beg your pardon," Molly said, trying to sound indignant. "You have no right to molest us—"

"Goddammit, get off your horses!" he said. "I ain't got time to fool with you. You come riding right on top of me, and now I've got to put you on ice."

Molly saw Buck's eyes stretched open in fear. She said quietly, "Do as he says," and swung down from the saddle. Buck did the same.

The bounty hunter moved toward them. Molly watched for her opportunity, and it came when he reached for their horses' reins. His gun swung away from her. She thrust a hand downward and pulled up her skirt. With her other hand she drew her derringer.

"Stop right there, mister," she said, leveling the two-shot derringer at him. "Drop your gun."

The man looked at her in alarm. He let the reins fall from his hand, but he did not release his revolver.

"Drop it," Molly ordered.

"You can shoot me with that little gun, lady," he said, "but you won't knock me off my feet. I'll get off a shot, and it'll take the boy."

Molly now saw that his gun was pointed toward Buck.

"Look, lady, I've got my back against the wall," he said. "I'm on the run and need money. If I don't collect that reward on Cole Estes, there ain't much in front of me. So I reckon you'd better drop that sneak gun."

Molly clenched her jaw. She sensed that he wasn't a man to bluff. She slowly lowered the derringer.

The shot that came from the hilltop behind her was thunderously loud. It knocked the bounty hunter off his feet, sending him sprawling back into the brush. The horses squealed and milled about.

Molly turned and looked up. Back-lighted against the morning sky was Pony Diehl. He aimed his long-barreled rifle down at them, sighting through the telescopic lens. He stood up there for several moments, then lowered the rifle and came down the hillside.

"Pony, you got him!" Buck exclaimed.

The bounty hunter lay still in the brush. A gaping hole was all that remained of his left eye.

Pony said, "Matt told me to make sure you two were gone." He casually inspected the corpse.

"You taking orders from him now?" Molly asked.

Pony straightened up and eyed her. "This killer followed you in here, lady. Matt was right—you bring trouble."

"No!" Buck exclaimed. "He didn't follow us. He knew where the cave was. He said he'd used it himself."

Pony cast a doubtful look at him.

"It's true," Buck said. "That's what he said."

"Nobody followed us, Pony," Molly said. "We watched our back trail and camped a long ways away from here before we rode to the cave."

Pony shrugged. "Well, I guess you two need to start riding again, don't you?"

Buck seemed surprised by the outlaw's hostility. He turned away and jogged after the horses. Molly walked after him, leaving Pony behind.

• • •

Molly and Buck rode back to Barnum and stayed the night in Miz Andrews' boardinghouse. She asked no questions, but was obviously curious, and Molly told her that Buck had found his father.

From Miz Andrews, Molly learned that Will Parlow was a fugitive. A district judge in Johnson County had issued a bench warrant for Will Parlow and all the men in the Union Pacific posse.

News of the burning of the Outlaw Ranch had brought a public outcry throughout the county unlike any since the famous invasion three years ago. Two of the men shot down by Parlow's posse were local cowhands with no known criminal records. Other corpses were too badly burned to be immediately identified, but whether they were criminals or not, the judge who issued the warrant asserted that the men had a right to surrender before being gunned down. Two witnesses against Parlow were Bar C cowhands who had been riding nearby when they sighted the grass fire.

Parlow's whereabouts were unknown. It was believed that he had taken his posse back to southern Wyoming and probably to Cheyenne, where U.P. attorneys could defend him.

Upon their return to Denver, Molly took Buck straight to Mrs. Boatwright. The three of them discussed the matter of the $120 Buck owed her and made an agreement. Buck would resume living in the basement room and work off the debt by doing chores and odd jobs around the boardinghouse.

Molly had Buck primed for this arrangement, and he quietly accepted it. The alternative of returning to the Mike Payton Home for Boys was unacceptable to him, so working here and going to the tutor every afternoon was the lesser of the evils.

Buck had sold his mare and saddle in Cheyenne for twelve dollars, and Molly was pleased to see him pull these crumpled bills out of his trouser pocket and

CHAPTER XXVIII

Back in her room at the hotel, Molly tried to calm Buck, with little success.

"Parlow's a murderer," Buck said, "but he's a free man. My father, who never killed anyone, is locked up and will probably be sentenced to twenty years in prison. It isn't right, Molly."

"Taking the law into your own hands isn't the answer, Buck," she said.

His jaw clenched when he said, "Somebody's got to do it."

"There's a better way," Molly said.

He looked at her doubtfully. "What?"

"Prove Parlow's guilty of killing Matt Bledsoe and of stealing the bank money from him," Molly said.

Buck's expression softened for a moment. "Can you do that?"

"I can try," Molly said.

Buck looked at her with increasing excitement and said, "We can search around and find the body of Matt Bledsoe. That'll prove Parlow's guilty."

For a moment Molly considered sending Buck into the hilly country south of town on a wild-goose chase that would keep him busy for several days. But then she shook her head, deciding she had better keep the boy in sight as much as possible. Left to his own devices, he might try to take on Will Parlow alone.

"When Parlow moved the corpse," Molly said, "he probably took it far from here, buried it deep, and concealed the grave. I don't think there's much chance of finding it."

"But what can we do?" Buck asked. "Without the body, there's no proof."

"You're forgetting the money," Molly said.

"What about it?" Buck asked.

"Thirty-seven thousand dollars is not easy to hide," Molly said. "Unless he's buried it somewhere, he has it with him."

Buck's eyes bugged open. "Where do we start looking? What if he sees us—?"

Molly smiled. "One thing at a time, Buck. The first thing we have to do is make sure he doesn't recognize us if he does see us."

Leaving Buck at the hotel, Molly went out shopping for clothes. In three-quarters of an hour she came back and spread her purchases out on the bed.

"I ain't going to dress up like a girl!" Buck exclaimed when he saw two dark wigs beside the new simple dresses and light cotton wraps.

"Then you'll have to stay here in the hotel," Molly said. "I can't take the risk of Parlow seeing you."

"I'll wear my sombrero and serape," Buck said quickly.

Molly shook her head. "I recognized you with your back turned."

"Damn," Buck muttered in frustration.

Faces and hands slightly colored by dark rouge, Molly and Buck left the hotel through a back entrance. The sun had set an hour and a half ago. The disguises might not have fooled anyone in full daylight, but by the pale light of evening Molly hoped that a bystander would see them only as two Mexican girls in long black dresses.

Molly had coached Buck to walk slowly and not stride out as he liked to do. Together they moved along one side of the plaza, as though on an evening stroll.

Molly noticed they attracted little attention from the clusters of people who laughed and talked in the center of the plaza. As they passed the front of a saloon, a cowhand came out and touched a hand to the brim of his hat.

" 'Evening, señoritas," he said.

They passed by, and Buck glanced at Molly, grinning.

"Fooled him," Buck said.

They left the plaza and walked two blocks farther, entering the street that ran past the rooming house Molly had seen Will Parlow enter. Most of the windows on the second floor were dark now.

"Is he there?" Buck asked.

Molly shook her head. "There's no light in his window. It's the second one from this end."

They crossed the street and went to the outside staircase that led up to the second floor of the frame boardinghouse. The steps creaked as Molly and Buck mounted them. At the top, she slowly turned the door handle and found it to be unlocked.

The door opened into a hallway. Molly stepped inside, and when Buck came in behind her, she whispered to him, "Stay here and keep a lookout."

"What if someone comes?" Buck asked.

"Rap twice on Parlow's door," Molly said, "and get out of here. We'll meet back at the hotel."

Buck nodded quickly and brushed stray hairs of the wig out of his eyes.

Molly moved down the hall to the second door. It was locked. As she knelt in front of it, she took out a ring of master skeleton keys from under her dress. The fourth one she tried in the keyhole released the lock.

Molly entered the darkened room, seeing the vague forms of an iron bedstead, a tall dresser, and a washstand; across the room was a curtained closet. She fired a match and touched it to the wick of a lamp on the washstand. She turned the wick down as low as she could without extinguishing the flame and moved to the dresser.

Molly quickly searched every drawer and found nothing but clothes and three boxes of ammunition—

two for a .45 Peacemaker and one for a .44 Winchester—and a pint bottle of patent medicine. Turning the label to the light, she read "Dr. King's Cure-All, a miracle medicine guaranteed to cure chronic flatulence, constipation, itching of the orifices, while cleansing the entire system."

Molly crossed the room to the closet and pulled the curtain aside. A heavy mackinaw hung from the rod in there, along with three shirts, two pairs of trousers, and a pin-striped suit. On the floor she saw an extra pair of boots and a leather grip.

Kneeling, Molly set the lamp on the floor and pulled the grip out. She released the two brass clasps and opened it. The bag was empty.

Disappointed, Molly started to close the grip, but then her eye was caught by a side pocket in the lining. She pulled the grip fully open and reached in. There, in the side pocket, almost concealed, were three bundles of fifty-dollar bills. Molly lifted one out. By lamplight she saw the blue bank wrapper around the greenbacks, stamped "Santos State Bank."

She kept the bundle and closed the grip, sliding it back beside the boots. She stood and closed the curtain. Turning around, she held the lamp up. The only object left in this room large enough to hold $37,000 was the bed.

Molly crossed the room to it and thrust her hand under the mattress. She felt the rough texture of the ticking, and a moment later was startled by two quick knocks on the door.

Molly straightened up and rushed across the room to the washstand. She set the lamp on it and blew out the flame. She went to the door and yanked it open. Buck was in the hall. In the near-darkness she saw a panicked look on his face.

"Parlow," he whispered. "He's coming—"

"Get out of here!" Molly snapped. She turned around and knelt in front of the door, hurriedly bringing out her ring of master skeleton keys. She locked the door and stood. Buck was still there.

"I won't leave you," he said.

Exasperated, Molly took him by the arm. They strode to the end of the hall. The outside door was open several inches, and as they reached it, Molly heard the stairs creaking under someone's weight.

A moment later the door opened, and Will Parlow nearly collided with them. He drew back a step.

"*Buenas noches, señor,*" Molly said in a low voice, ducking her head.

"Well, pardon me, ladies," Parlow replied. He made room for them to pass.

Molly and Buck stepped through the doorway and descended the staircase. Behind them, Molly heard the door close after Parlow entered the hallway. Buck swore softly in relief, and when they reached the bottom of the stairs, they hurried across the yard to the street. A dog barked at them until they reached the street that led to the plaza.

Back at the hotel, Molly showed the bundle of fifties to Buck. His eyes widened.

"He stole it! There's the proof!"

"This is enough proof for me," Molly said. "First thing in the morning, we'll find out if it's enough for Marshal Ayers."

But before sunrise in the morning Molly was awakened by repeated loud knocks on the door of her room. Upon answering, she was taken into custody by a deputy. So was Buck, who arrived at the jailhouse in handcuffs. There they learned from another deputy that Marshal Ayers was out with a posse. During the night, Cole Estes had escaped.

CHAPTER XXIX

"Look, lady, I've been slugged in the head and up the whole damned night, and I sure as hell ain't going to put up with any trouble from you."

Deputy Harker's head was bandaged, and his eyes were bloodshot. His voice was high-pitched when he spoke again.

"Now, just go along peaceful," he said, pointing toward the stairs to the cellblock, "and when Marshal Ayers gets back, you can tell your story to him."

Molly glanced at Buck. The boy stared at her, wide-eyed. She had lost her temper when she learned that Ayers had left word with his night jailer to lock her up, along with Buck. Ayers had no proof they were guilty of anything, but evidently was convinced one or both of them had engineered Cole's escape.

"All right," Molly said at last, "but I want to talk to Ayers the minute he gets back to Santos."

"Sure, sure," Harker said, motioning for the deputy to take her and Buck into detention rooms to be searched. Harker had explained to Molly that she would be strip-searched by a matron prior to being locked up in a cell upstairs.

The day passed with agonizing slowness. Molly was alone in a cell for women, separated from the men's cellblock by a plaster wall. She worried about Buck, even though the boy assured her that he "could take it."

Long after dark, Marshal Ayers walked into the women's cellblock. Molly stood when she saw him coming. She had stored up a good supply of outrage, and now she was prepared to share it with him. But as he stopped in front of her cell, obviously tired and dusty from a long ride, another thought came to her.

"Did you catch him?" she asked.

Ayers shook his head. "The posse is still out. They'll pick up the trail tomorrow."

"Parlow in your posse?" Molly asked.

Ayers studied her. "For a time, he was."

"He's playing you like a fish on a line," Molly said.

The marshal stiffened. "What're you talking about?"

"Let Buck and me out of here," she said, "and we'll show you."

"You're not going anywhere," Ayers said, "until we get this thing straightened out."

"You can't hold us," Molly said.

"I can," he said, "and I will. You've both been charged with robbery and aiding a prisoner's escape. Your hearing will be in the morning."

Molly stared at him in amazement. "What proof do you have? Or is this just a theory of yours?"

"At first it was a theory," Ayers said with a tired smile. "But a search of your room gave me the evidence. You were careless with that bundle of fifty-dollar bills from the bank robbery. You were in on that from the start, weren't you?"

"Last evening I got that bundle out of Will Parlow's room," Molly said. "I was going to bring it to you this morning."

Ayers cast a skeptical look at her.

"I can prove it," Molly said. "I know where the rest of the thirty-seven thousand is."

"Are you confessing?" Ayers asked.

"You're not even listening to me," Molly said. "Parlow confessed to me."

Ayers shrugged. "So tell me. Where is the money?"

"Stuffed in a mattress in his room," Molly said. "I didn't actually see it, but I felt the bundles of money. Take me there, and I'll show you."

Ayers shook his head. "The only place I'm taking

you is to a courtroom in the morning." He turned to leave.

"At least go to Parlow's room," Molly said, "and look for yourself. I'm telling you the truth."

Ayers paused, then nodded once. "All right, I'll have a look. At least this will be a shorter wild-goose chase than the last one you led me on."

Molly watched him go, then paced in her cell for half an hour until Ayers returned. She met him at the barred door.

"Parlow's gone," Ayers said, studying Molly's face as he spoke. "Moved out."

Molly slapped her hand down on the steel crosspiece of the cell door. "He's a step ahead of me again."

"The owner of the rooming house was pretty unhappy," Ayers went on. "Parlow left without paying for the mattress."

"What?" Molly demanded.

"The mattress in his room was ruined," Ayers said, "cut from one end to the other." Reaching into his trouser pocket, he pulled out half a dozen blue bank wrappers. "He must have been in a hurry. He left these behind in the mattress. I reckon I owe you an apology—you and the boy."

Molly watched with mounting excitement as Ayers brought out his jailer's key and unlocked the cell door. He opened it and stepped aside.

"Parlow sprung Cole Estes out of jail," Molly said as she left the cell. "He did it to throw you off his trail."

Ayers nodded. "I figured that out when I stepped into his room and saw the mattress. He's the one who slugged Harker early this morning."

"What about Cole?" Molly asked.

"Cole was probably asleep when Parlow went up there and opened his cell," Ayers said. "It was dark, anyway, and Cole couldn't have seen who did it."

"Parlow could have killed him right there," Molly said.

Ayers nodded. "A fugitive Cole Estes was worth

more to him." He added, "Maybe Parlow was laying for him somewhere outside of Santos. That's his way."

Molly kept this theory to herself when she walked with Buck back to El Castillo Hotel. He was excited about the fact that Marshal Ayers had discovered the truth about Will Parlow and now believed them. Buck did not conceal his happiness over the fact that Cole Estes was a free man.

"I'll never see my father again," Buck confided to her as they came to the hotel. "I know that. He's headed for the border. He'll go to South America, where no rewards are hanging over his head, and he'll live in peace down there."

Buck paused. "I'm glad I got to know him, Molly. He's a good man in his own way."

Molly nodded and smiled. Once again she caught a glimpse of the man in him. "Just like his son," she said.

Over a late supper in the hotel restaurant, Buck speculated in his rapid-fire way that his father would become an important man in South America, perhaps the owner of a huge cattle ranch or even a national leader.

After the meal, Molly walked with him back to his room, then retraced her steps to the door of her room. She unlocked it and stepped inside, sensing immediately that she was not alone.

An instant later a strong arm encircled her waist. She reacted instinctively. Shifting her weight, she kicked back one foot. The heel of her high button shoe struck the man's shin.

"Ow!" he cried out.

Molly twisted away, bent down, and drove an elbow into him.

"Damn!" he howled. "Stop hitting me! I was only trying to keep you from shooting me."

Molly quickly shut the door and turned around. "I thought you were Parlow."

"No, it's just me," Cole Estes said, breathing hard.

CHAPTER XXX

"Oh, Cole," Molly whispered, stepping into his arms. "Why didn't you leave Santos?"

He held her tightly. "I was lucky to get this far. I never got a look at who opened my cell, but when I went downstairs and saw that jailer stretched out on the floor, I figured it out. Parlow wanted me to run. That would leave him with the money."

"What did you do?" Molly asked.

"I ran," Cole said, "but not the way he figured. The front door of the jailhouse was open, and a horse was tied at the rail out there. I backed up, and let myself out through a back window. I hid out in an alley for a couple hours, then made my way to the plaza. Buck had told me you were staying at El Castillo, and I was looking for a way to get to your room. At daybreak a Mexican saw me, and I described you and the boy and told him I had to see you. Well, he put two and two together and offered to hide me. Said he'd do it as a favor to you."

"Esteban," Molly said.

"That's right," Cole said. "From the news around town, he'd figured out why you were here. Your room was paid for, and we decided that was the best place for me to hide until we could get news of what happened to you and Buck at the marshal's office."

"Cole," Molly said, taking his hand in hers, "it's too dangerous for you to stay here any longer."

"Just awhile longer," he whispered. He put his other hand behind her neck and pulled her to him. His lips found hers. They kissed long and passionately, pressing against one another. Molly felt her arousal swell up inside her, building like a head of steam in an engine.

Cole pulled back and unbuttoned her dress. Molly stepped out of it, and he caressed her while she slipped off her underclothes.

"Cole . . ." she whispered. Molly found the bed in the darkness of the room. She lay down and waited for him, listening to the whisper of cloth on skin as he undressed. That soft sound and the anticipation of the man was powerfully erotic to her. By the time he came to the bed her desire was running at full speed, her body silently shouting for him.

Later they lay on the bed together, near but not touching. Molly contentedly listened to his breathing and closed her eyes. She slept, but quickly awakened when he sat up in bed and swung his legs over the side.

"Cole," she whispered.

He murmured a reply as he bent down and found his clothes on the floor beside the bed.

Molly raised up on an elbow. In the darkness of the room she could not see Cole, but she heard him pull on his clothes.

"How will you escape?" she asked.

"I'll get a horse and ride for Mexico," he replied.

"A posse is out there," Molly said. She added, "Parlow might be, too."

"That posse has been out a long time," Cole said. "Those men are saddle-sore and tired by now." He added, "I can figure a posse."

"Parlow's different," Molly said.

"Maybe it's time I met the man," he said. He came to her and leaned down and kissed her. "One day, things will cool off. The U.P. will withdraw that reward. Lawmen and bounty hunters will forget about me. I'll come back. Tell the kid I'll hunt him up." He kissed her again. "And you."

He left. Molly heard the door open and close. The room was suddenly quiet and empty.

Molly sat up. She got out of bed and lit a lamp. A plan had formed in her mind, and she went over it while she pulled on her riding clothes.

Cole would ride through the hill country south of Santos. She would follow at a distance. If Will Parlow was out there waiting, she would have a chance to bring him in—along with the money.

CHAPTER XXXI

Molly's plan did not include Buck, but as she strode down the lamplit hall of the hotel, she heard bare feet padding behind her. She looked over her shoulder and saw the boy running to catch up. He wore only his underwear.

"Molly, what're you doing?" he asked. "Where're you going?"

She stopped and turned around. "The question is, why are you awake at this time of night?"

"I can't sleep," Buck said. "I'm all churned up inside. I heard a couple doors open and close, and I looked out in the hall and saw you." He looked at her. "This has something to do with my father, doesn't it? You're going to meet him."

Molly shook her head. "Go back to bed, Buck."

"No, I'm riding with you," he said. His jaw was set. "You can't stop me, Molly. You know where my father is, don't you?"

"No, I don't, Buck," she said. They looked at one another, and she thought about all they had been through together. And Buck was right. She could not prevent him from following her.

"All right," she said at last. "Get dressed."

They rode out of Santos to the south as day was breaking. Molly set a fast pace, and in a short while she saw that they had closed the distance. A rider was in the hills ahead, and when Molly picked him up in her field glasses, she saw that he was Cole Estes.

"We can catch up!" Buck exclaimed.

Molly shook her head. "Not now."

"Why?" he demanded.

"Do as I tell you," Molly said. She spurred her horse. "We'll keep him in sight."

Cole Estes was riding at a slow pace, and as Molly drew a tight rein on her horse, she wondered why. Perhaps he was saving the horse's strength in case a posse cut his trail. But the answer came as the sky brightened with the rising sun.

Molly saw another set of hoofprints, and the trail of a pack animal. Cole was following someone. As the trail veered toward the spring Esteban had led her to, she thought she knew. Cole was hunting the hunter—Will Parlow.

Half an hour later Molly lost sight of Cole in the piñon- and cedar-covered hills. When she neared the spring, she slowed and studied the surrounding terrain. The trail led straight south, but the clumps of trees could easily hide a man.

"What's the matter?" Buck asked in a low voice.

Molly shrugged. She rode on slowly until she reached the base of the hill overlooking the spring. Reining to a halt in the draw at the bottom of the low hill, she turned in the saddle and touched a finger to her lips, then dismounted.

Molly climbed the slope. Taking off her Stetson, she crawled to the top and looked down at the spring. A riderless horse was there.

"What the hell do you think you're doing?"

Startled, Molly cut her gaze to a clump of trees a dozen yards to her left and saw Cole stand up. He came around the trees and strode angrily to her.

He demanded again, "What the hell do you think you're doing?"

"I know what I'm doing, Cole," Molly said evenly. "You don't need to yell at me."

Buck came riding up the hill to them. He led Molly's horse. Cole's expression slowly softened as he looked at the boy, and then he swore in exasperation.

"I'm after Parlow," Molly said.

"And you figure you'll find him if you keep me in sight," Cole said.

Molly nodded.

"Well, I'm on his trail, for a change," Cole said.

Buck swore excitedly.

"But if I spotted you," Cole said, "Parlow will, too."

Gunfire erupted, and dirt sprayed at their feet. The horses reared, and Molly dived for cover. She saw Cole do the same, and as more shots were fired, Buck spilled out of the saddle of his rearing horse.

Molly heard Cole cursing, and she rose to see Buck lying on his back, eyes bugged open.

"Are you hurt?" she called out.

He gasped for air, and Molly realized the wind had been knocked out of him. He rolled over, and more shots came from a distant rifle.

"Find cover!" Molly shouted at the boy. She saw him roll down the slope, out of the line of fire. No blood was on his clothes. She felt relieved that he had not been shot.

Molly crawled along the opposite slope of the hill to a clump of trees Cole was using as cover. He peered through the branches, trying to locate the rifleman. Molly moved up beside him.

"Damn," Cole said. "I need Pony, need him bad."

Cole pointed through the screen of piñon branches to a clump of cedars nearly a hundred yards away. "The second volley came from those trees. But he's moving. I saw him run. He's probably trying to get behind us."

Molly looked around. She saw the thick growth of brush and small trees down in the draw by the spring, and behind her was a rock outcropping.

"There's two of us," she said. "If we split up, we might catch him in a crossfire."

Cole looked at her in surprise. "Yeah?" His eyes went to the revolver in her hand. The midday sun reflected off the nickel-plated frame. "You can use that thing?"

Molly replied with a nod of her head. "Cover me. I'll run straight back to those rocks. Then I'll cover you while you move down to the spring. If we haven't drawn him out by then, we can work our way up that slope." She pointed to the hill beyond the spring.

Cole stared at her while she spoke. "You're telling me what we're going to do?"

"I'm giving you a plan," Molly said. "Do you have a better one?"

"No," he said slowly, "I reckon I don't."

Molly turned. In one swift motion, like a foot racer, she rose and ran for the rock outcropping. She had almost reached it when she heard the deep *boom, boom, boom* of a rifle, and bullets sang past her, splattering into the rocks.

She bent low as she ran, then ducked her head and rolled on one shoulder. Coming to rest beside the outcropping, she scurried behind it. She lay there, breathing hard, listening to the loud popping sounds that told her Cole was returning fire. His shots were answered by the rifle again.

From this protected position, Molly could look down into the draw where she had last seen Buck. Now she edged over far enough to see him. He held the reins of their horses and looked up at her with a fearful expression. Molly signaled him to stay there.

Peering over the top of the rock outcropping, she saw Cole looking back at her. He motioned toward a clump of cedars off to his right, then turned and fired two shots into it.

The cedars were within pistol range, and Molly took aim. As Cole sprinted away, she fired, spacing her shots from one side of the lowest branches to the other. Cole ran downslope, finding cover behind a tree and some brush near the muddy bank of the spring. No rifle fire came this time.

Molly reloaded, wondering if the rifleman had been hit. As she snapped the cylinder shut, her question was answered by a volley of booming shots. This volley did not come from the clump of cedars she and

Cole had fired into. Then Molly glimpsed a flash of movement on the hilltop beyond those trees. She stood and ran down into the draw.

"Over there," Molly said, pointing toward the hilltop. "He just ran over the next hill."

Molly ran past him, around the spring, and up the side of the draw.

"Not so damned fast," Cole said, coming up behind her. "You might run straight into him."

She slowed, and they came to the top side by side, peering over it. The next hill was like the others, rounded at the crest and dotted with piñon trees and clumps of cedars.

"He's on the other side," Molly whispered.

Cole studied the terrain, shaking his head. "I don't like this."

"Maybe we should split up again," Molly said, "and wait him out."

Cole did not reply, but his jaw was set as he looked at the crest of the next hill.

"The longer we wait here," Molly said, "the more time we give him to take a better position."

"You're right about that," Cole said. "Wait here."

Before Molly could argue, Cole jumped to his feet and sprinted away, running hard toward a stand of piñon trees on the side of the next hill. He was met by a lone rifleman who stepped out from behind those trees. Will Parlow held his Winchester in his hands.

Cole halted and quickly raised his revolver. Molly saw Parlow grin as he shot from the hip, and Cole was spun around by the impact of the bullet. He went down, sprawling into the dirt. Parlow jacked another round into the chamber. He raised the rifle to his shoulder, taking aim at the prone figure of Cole Estes.

CHAPTER XXXII

Molly held her revolver in both hands, looking at Will Parlow over the sights. She squeezed the trigger.

Parlow was rocked back by the .38 slug, a look of surprise sweeping over his face. Molly fired again, and the rifle fell from his hands. Parlow sank to his knees and fell forward, his face banging into the dirt.

"Cole!" Molly shouted, springing to her feet. She ran to him, seeing a splotch of blood on his shirtfront. Twenty yards away, Parlow lay still. The brass shell casing ejected from his rifle was beside him, glinting in the sunlight.

Molly knelt beside Cole. He looked up at her.

"The bastard shot me," he said.

Pulling away his shirt, Molly saw that his wound was high on his chest, below the shoulder.

"You'll live through this one," she said.

"Molly! Molly!"

She looked back and saw Buck running over the crest of the hill. He dodged a growth of brush and came at them, running hard. For an instant Molly was reminded of the first time she had seen him. After frightening the bear away, he had come running toward her, shouting.

In that instant, Molly understood why Buck reminded her of her brother, Chick. The two were the same age, caught between childhood and adulthood, and Chick had come running across a yard to her, urgently calling her name. Molly had swept him up in her arms and told him everything was going to be all right. And it was. They had grown up on their own, depending on each other, and had gone on to lead the lives they had chosen for themselves.

Buck halted several paces away. He came forward tentatively.

"Come here," Cole said. "I'm not hit bad, thanks to Molly."

Buck tried to smile. He came to his father and knelt beside him. "You're bleeding," he whispered.

"Soon as I get a bandage on," Cole said, "I'll be ready to ride."

Molly left them and went to Will Parlow. She turned the body over. His eyes stared up at the sky, seeing nothing. Her first bullet had struck the base of his neck, and her second had hit him in the chest.

Molly stood and walked to the top of the hill. In the next draw Parlow's horse and pack animal were tied to a piñon pine. She realized their game of hide and seek had ended when she and Cole had unknowingly come close to the horses. More than anything, Parlow feared losing them.

Molly hiked down there and confirmed what she suspected. Hidden with supplies in the panniers on the pack animal were bundles of cash from the Santos State Bank and sacks of gold coins from the Union Pacific robbery.

Leading the horse and pack animal over the hill, Molly found Cole alone, sitting up now.

"I sent Buck after my horse," he said. With a pained grin he added, "The kid told me you'd fix me up better than any sawbones could."

Molly knelt beside him and took off his shirt. She tore away a clean piece of it and mopped the wound. At close range, the rifle slug had cleanly passed through him.

She wrapped the torn shirt around his chest and over his other shoulder, tying it tight.

"That'll hold the bleeding," Molly said, "until you come back to Santos and see a doctor."

Cole looked at her. "That boy thinks a lot of you, Molly."

"He thinks more of his father," she said. "He talks about you all the time."

Cole shook his head. "But he didn't shout my name when he came running over here." Cole put on his hat and stood.

Molly helped him to his feet, and for a moment they stood close together, looking into each other's eyes.

"I wish things could have been different," he said.

"Come back to Santos with me, Cole," Molly said. "With the money returned, the heat will be off you."

Buck returned, leading Cole's saddle horse. The boy held the reins while Cole grabbed the saddle horn, put his boot in the stirrup, and swung up, grimacing.

"So long," he said. He turned the horse to the south and rode off.

Molly knew she could stop him, but she watched him go. She looked at Buck and saw the boy blinking against his tears. When Cole topped a hill and rode out of sight, he turned to her.

"Let's go back to Denver," he said.

Stephen Overholser was born in Bend, Oregon, the middle son of Western author, Wayne D. Overholser. Convinced, in his words, that "there was more to learn outside of school than inside," he left Colorado State College in his senior year. He was drafted and served in the U.S. Army in Vietnam. Following his discharge, he launched his career as a writer, publishing three short stories in *Zane Grey Western Magazine*. On a research visit to the University of Wyoming at Laramie, he came across an account of a shocking incident that preceded the Johnson County War in Wyoming in 1892. It was this incident that became the inspiration for his first novel, *A Hanging at Sweetwater* (1974), that received the Spur Award from the Western Writers of America. *Molly and the Confidence Man* (1975) followed, the first in a series of books about Molly Owens, a clever, resourceful, and tough undercover operative working for a fictional detective agency in the Old West. Among the most notable of Stephen Overholser's later titles are *Search for the Fox* (1976) and *Track of a Killer* (1982). Stephen Overholser's latest novel is *Dark Embers at Dawn*.

give them to Mrs. Boatwright as the first payment on the "loan."

Later Mrs. Boatwright confided to Molly that Esther Raines was none the wiser. She was happy now that her money and purse had been returned, and her door was secured with a new lock.

The next morning Molly wired a message to Horace Fenton. She told her employer that her wounds had healed, and she was ready for a new assignment.

In the following days, while Molly waited for his reply, she read in the Denver papers about the storm of protests in Wyoming over the Hole-in-the-Wall killings. Accusations were thrown back and forth between northern and southern Wyoming, and a court battle was brewing around Will Parlow's refusal to return to Johnson County. Parlow had been seen in both Cheyenne and Laramie and was reported to be living in high style inside a private railroad car owned by the Union Pacific.

Parlow himself waged a shadowy battle through the Wyoming newspapers. He claimed that he and his men were a legal posse in pursuit of desperate criminals and had acted responsibly. He cited at length his record as a peace officer in New Mexico and said his services were much appreciated in the whole Southwest.

Parlow predicted that he would be murdered if he ever set foot in northern Wyoming. In the pages of the Cheyenne *Leader*, he made vague accusations that the citizens in that part of the state knowingly protected notorious outlaws like Cole Estes.

Molly read these "accounts" and wondered if Will Parlow knew that when she and Buck left Barnum they had ridden to Buffalo, Wyoming. In the county courthouse, they had given a deposition to the court clerk, a complete account of what they had witnessed at the compound of cabins known as the Outlaw Ranch.

When the Fenton assignment came from New York, Molly read it with dismay. This was not the sort of work she liked. Horace Fenton told her to contact a

Fenton operative in Denver named William Reynolds and assist him in a divorce case. She was to follow the wife.

Molly did so, and passed the hours of idle time while waiting for the woman to come out of a dress shop or the home of a friend by reading newspapers. The storm of protests spread into neighboring states and raised a fundamental question about law and order in the West. Most newspaper editors railed against "vigilantes and bounty hunters," but a few hailed the courage of "deputized lawmen" doing battle with the "outlaw element."

The mighty Union Pacific Railroad finally broke its silence and took most of the steam out of the controversy by disbanding the posse. Will Parlow was released from employment. He quickly dropped from sight.

The matter ended with a flurry of accusations that Parlow had been spirited out of the state rather than let him face a murder charge in Johnson County. This was an allegation the Union Pacific vigorously denied.

Molly kept odd hours while working on her new assignment with William Reynolds, but she managed to speak to Mrs. Boatwright frequently. She learned that Buck was living up to his end of the agreement.

"I've never seen a boy read newspapers like he does," Mrs. Boatwright said. "He reads every word he can find about outlaws, even in *The Police Gazette*."

"He's looking for news about his father," Molly said.

"Well, he isn't finding anything," Mrs. Boatwright said. "The other day he told me his father was probably in South America by now."

"I wish I could believe that," Molly said. "It isn't good for Buck to have Cole Estes on his mind all the time." Molly could have said the same thing about herself. She had been thinking about him a great deal too, hoping he would somehow get to Denver.

The suspicious husband who had hired the Fenton agency was much disappointed when Molly reported that his estranged wife was not seeing another man. He confided to Reynolds that women are inclined to protect one another, and a man should be given the case. Molly was released.

Eight days later, while Molly awaited a new assignment from Horace Fenton, the newspapers were filled with news of the Cole Estes gang. The trio had robbed a bank in Santos, New Mexico. Pony Diehl had been killed in a shoot-out, and Matt Bledsoe had escaped with most of the money, over $37,000 in cash. Cole Estes himself had been captured.

The next day, Buck was gone.

CHAPTER XXIII

"I don't know, I just don't know about that boy," Mrs. Boatwright said. She stood in the doorway of Molly's room and watched her pack clothes into her valise on the bed. "Maybe you ought to let him go. Maybe he needs to be out on his own long enough to get good and lonely and hungry, and then he'll want to come back."

Molly closed the valise and straightened up.

"Anyhow," Mrs. Boatwright went on, "you can't be chasing after him every time he takes a notion to run off. He didn't steal anything this time—except he still owes me money."

"I think I know where he went," Molly said, lifting the valise off the bed, "and if I'm right, Buck needs help. Or he needs someone to stop him."

"Stop him?" Mrs. Boatwright asked in alarm. "Say, this has something to do with Cole Estes, doesn't it?"

Molly carried her bag to the door. As she moved past Mrs. Boatwright, she said, "I'll be able to tell you when I get back from New Mexico."

The afternoon southbound train took her to Trinidad in southern Colorado. She stayed overnight there, and early in the morning boarded a shiny red Concord stagecoach that headed south, crossing the state line at Raton Pass.

In the seat beside her sat a dark-skinned girl with a baby in her arms. A hardware and dry-goods salesman sat in the seat across from her, dozing, his hands laced around his ample belly. His head bobbed with the motion of the stagecoach.

The road switchbacked down the New Mexico side of the mountain. Molly looked out the window of the coach and saw the hilly landscape. The hills were speckled with piñon pines and from this panoramic view appeared dry and uninhabited.

But appearances proved to be deceiving. As the coach reached the bottom and wound through the hills, Molly saw small fields of corn, cattle grazing in the shallow valleys, and bands of sheep herded by Mexican boys and panting dogs.

A stage station was in a village nestled in these hills. The adobe houses were built around a white-washed Catholic church. Strings of red chili peppers hung from many of these houses, adding bright color to the adobe walls that were the color of creamed coffee.

At the stage station Molly shared a table with the drummer. He was a talkative man, but Molly only half-listened to his droning voice while she ate goat stew and tortillas. The meal was followed by a dessert of *flan*, a custard covered with a light caramel sauce.

Afterward Molly stretched her legs by walking around the village while a fresh team of six horses was hitched to the Concord. Children played on the dusty streets, and a few men wearing wide-brimmed sombreros stood in patches of shade.

The day passed with the stagecoach following a long valley out of the hills, passing scattered *ranchitos*. Molly saw more adobe houses, and more children. She caught a mood of peacefulness here, of human warmth. Shortly before nightfall, the stage rolled into Santos, and the drummer awakened long enough to bid Molly a loud good-bye.

Santos was a mixture of the old and the new. Adobe buildings with stone walks were built around the town plaza. Within this square were tall trees and trimmed bushes and flowerbeds, a marble fountain, and many benches. These were used by the townspeople on evening strolls.

Beyond the plaza, to the west, were newer buildings. In measured residential blocks in this section of town, Molly saw fine homes of stone and brick, embraced by white picket fences. A gold mill had recently opened near Santos, bringing in new residents and a measure of prosperity.

The iron-tired wheels of the stagecoach clattered loudly on the cobbled Calle de Plaza as the vehicle came down the street to the town square. The driver drew up in front of El Castillo Hotel. A bellman came out.

El Castillo was a low rambling adobe building, showing many additions in its one-hundred-year history. Spanish influence in the architecture took the form of one fortresslike turret of stone on the front corner of the building.

The hotel bellman was a handsome Mexican, a man in his sixties with streaks of silver in his black hair. As he greeted Molly, his thin mustache was raised by a broad smile. His uniform was a white shirt open at the collar, black trousers, and sandals on his feet.

"You will stay with us, señorita?" he asked, opening the door of the stagecoach.

Molly smiled as he helped her down. "Yes."

"*Bueno, muy bueno*," he said, quickly moving to the rear of the Concord, where the driver was lifting luggage out of the boot. He pointed to Molly's valise, and the bellman picked it up.

Molly followed him into the hotel. She found the lobby to be elegantly furnished with Spanish-style furniture, dark and large pieces, an Indian rug on the floor, and a brass chandelier overhead. She registered at the desk, and then followed the bellman down a long, dimly lighted hall. He unlocked the door to one of the rooms and led the way in.

The room was small and simply furnished. Across from the bed stood a washstand with a pitcher of water and an enameled basin. On the far wall was a clothes closet behind a colorful hand-woven blanket suspended from the ceiling. An Indian rug was on the floor.

After the bellman set her valise on a stand at the foot of the bed, Molly tipped him with a silver dollar. The man's brown eyes widened.

"*Gracias, señorita,*" he said, backing slowly toward the door. He paused there a moment, head slightly bowed, then looked up at her and said, "If you need anything, call for Esteban."

He turned rather quickly and started to leave, as though fearing his offer of friendship had been misinterpreted and he had offended her.

"Perhaps you can help me," Molly said.

Esteban stopped in the doorway and looked at her. "*Qué?*"

"I'm looking for a fourteen-year-old boy," Molly said. "He's slender with reddish hair. I don't know what he's wearing—"

"*Sí!*" Esteban exclaimed. "I think I have seen this *muchacho* with red hair! He was on the plaza."

"When?" Molly asked.

Esteban paused, thinking. "I believe . . . two days ago. I have not seen him since."

"Do you have any idea where he might have gone?" Molly asked.

Esteban shrugged, shaking his head sympathetically. "This *muchacho*, he is your brother? Your son?"

"No," Molly replied, "a friend." She paused. "One more question, Esteban. Where is the Santos jail?"

The Mexican's eyes narrowed. "One block from here, *señorita*." He gestured toward the front door of El Castillo. "Walk down Calle de Plaza one block. You will see a stone building with flagpoles above the door. The marshal is there, and the jail is upstairs." He gave her a worried look. "I hope your young friend is not there."

"So do I, Esteban," Molly said.

After he was gone, she went to the bed and sat down. The feather mattress beckoned her with a soft invitation that was almost irresistible. She was tired from two days of traveling and knew that if she lay down, she could sleep through the evening and the entire night.

She pushed away from the bed and stood. Taking off her dusty clothes, she unhooked her brassiere and then bent forward and slid her panties over her rounded hips and down her thighs. She let them fall to the floor and stepped out of them. She slid a toe under them, and with a deft kick she tossed the panties onto the heap of clothes on the bed.

Naked, Molly went to the washstand and dampened a handcloth. She washed her body, feeling an erotic sensation as the wet cloth passed over her creamy skin. Then, after combing out her hair, she put on fresh clothes, a serge dress with lace trim at the sleeves and neck.

After eating a light supper in El Castillo's restaurant, Molly followed Esteban's directions to the city jailhouse. She found it. The building was massive, two-story, and built of quarried granite.

Molly climbed the short flight of steps to the thick double doors and decided this was a public building constructed in the spirit of revolution. She grasped the brass handle of one door and pulled it open.

The large room she entered smelled of cigar smoke. She saw the source. Behind a desk across the room sat a deputy, feet up, with a stubby cigar sticking out of his mouth. He looked over his boots at Molly. "Howdy, ma'am," he said as she approached.

"Are you the marshal?" Molly asked.

He spoke around the cigar. "Nope, I'm the night jailer." He eyed her and said, "Anything I can do for you, Miss . . . ?"

"I'm here to see Cole Estes," she said. "My name is Molly Owens."

He swung his feet down from the desk. "Name's Deputy Harker. Plenty of people want a look at the famous Cole Estes. There's been a regular parade of folks coming in here for a look, and when I turn them away, they head out in the country to see the spot

where the Estes gang was shot up." He gave her a deliberate once-over. "Just what's your business with Mr. Cole Estes?"

"I'm looking for his son," she said.

Harker's jaw dropped open. "Son? Cole Estes has a son? Are you his . . . wife?"

"No," Molly said.

"Well, maybe you'd better explain—"

"I'll explain everything to the marshal of Santos," Molly said.

"Marshal Ayers ain't here tonight," Harker said. "He's at home, where he can't be bothered, 'cept for emergencies."

"This might be one," Molly said.

Harker stared at her.

"Deputy," Molly said, "if the marshal wants to see me tonight, tell him I'm at El Castillo Hotel."

Molly turned and strode across the room toward the big double doors. She did not know if the deputy would relay her message tonight, but she had confirmed the one thing she wanted to know: Cole Estes was still in Santos, locked in a cell upstairs. The next problem was to find Buck.

In the gathering darkness outside, Molly followed the boardwalk back to the plaza. Night sounds reached her, and a ripple of laughter came from a brightly lighted saloon ahead. As she neared the batwing doors, two men came out. They spoke briefly, then parted.

Molly quickly turned away, ducking into a darkened doorway. The man walking out to his horse tied at the rail was Will Parlow.

CHAPTER XXIV

From the night shadows of the recessed doorway, Molly watched Parlow lead his horse down the street. Seeing his low-crowned, narrow-brimmed hat, she could not mistake the man, and Molly now realized that her first warning had been the distinct sound of his grating voice.

She stepped out onto the boardwalk and watched Parlow lead his horse into a livery half a block away. Presently, he came out and walked farther down the street, rounding the corner. Molly followed.

Molly came around the corner of the residential block in time to see the shadowy form of Parlow crossing the street. He went to a long, frame two-story rooming house. In the lamplight streaming out of windows, Molly saw him mount the outside staircase and enter the second-floor hall. Moments later, a light flickered and brightened in the second window from the end.

Molly hurried back to the plaza and El Castillo. She had been in her room only a quarter of an hour when a knock came at the door. Molly opened it to find a ruggedly handsome man with a bushy mustache. A badge was pinned to his vest. "Miss Owens?" he asked.

"Yes," Molly said. "You must be Marshal Ayers."

He nodded curtly, studying her. "What's this about the son of Cole Estes coming to Santos?"

"It's a long story, marshal," Molly said. "Come in, and I'll tell it to you."

In her room, Molly identified herself as an operative for the Fenton Investigative Agency and filled in Ayers on Buck's background. She did not go into detail about her pursuit of Cole Estes, but when she mentioned the name of Will Parlow, she saw a change of expression in the marshal's face—not a pleasant one.

"Parlow intercepted the Cole Estes gang outside of town," Ayers said. "He stopped them cold. I reckon we're indebted to him for that."

"Parlow has quite a reputation as a peace officer in this state, from what I hear," Molly said.

"Peace officer," Ayers repeated. He paused. "Miss Owens, saying a word against the name of Will Parlow is about the same as talking against motherhood. All through the Southwest, Parlow has gunned down plenty of outlaws. In a lawless time, he was the law."

Molly met the marshal's gaze when he paused again. Clearly, Ayers disliked Parlow and was confiding his thoughts to a stranger. Sometimes that was easier than speaking frankly to a neighbor.

"Times have changed," Ayers went on, "but Parlow hasn't. He still shoots from ambush, and up in Wyoming I hear he may have gunned down a few innocent men. Parlow doesn't know the law. He doesn't know the niceties of arrest procedures, and he probably doesn't much care about them. He has his way of working, and he's not a man to change." The marshal finished with a shake of his head.

"I want to talk to Cole Estes," Molly said.

"What for?" Ayers asked.

"To tell him his son is in Santos," Molly said.

"You think that boy will do something foolish," Ayers asked, "like try to bust his father out of my jail?"

Molly nodded.

"Nobody's going to bust Estes out," Ayers said, "especially not some kid."

"Buck is no ordinary kid," Molly said. "And I don't think Cole wants him to try it any more than you do.

If he knew Buck was here, Cole might try to get a message to him—one I could deliver."

"How?" Ayers asked.

"By posting a notice," Molly said, "or in the newspaper, perhaps."

Ayers considered this, and stood. "All right, I'll let you into the cellblock first thing in the morning."

Molly ate a breakfast of *huevos rancheros* in the hotel restaurant, and walked to the jailhouse with a *jalapeño* fire smoldering in her stomach. Inside the granite building, she was met by Marshal Ayers. He led her up a flight of iron stairs to a barred door. The door opened into a passageway between two rows of cells.

"I won't let you into his cell," Ayers said as he unlocked the barred door, "and I'll stay with you as long as you're in the cellblock."

"But I need to talk to him alone, marshal," Molly said.

Ayers stepped into the passageway after her and locked the door. "Well," he said, turning around, "I reckon I can wait down here where I can see you without hearing you."

Molly followed him to Cole's cell, realizing that the lawman did not fully trust her. Downstairs he had asked her to leave her handbag at the jailer's desk, but he had not searched her. A cautious lawman, Ayers had no intention of letting her out of his sight.

The other prisoners, Molly noticed, were Mexicans and Indians and several whites. They sat or reclined on thin straw mattresses spread over steel bunks. Many rose up to look at her as she passed by.

Two-thirds of the way down the passageway, Molly saw Cole Estes. Alone in the cell, he sat on his bunk with his back toward her. The prisoner in the next cell, a bearded man dressed in prison clothes, lay on his back, snoring.

Cole turned as he heard footfalls, and surprise registered on his face when he saw Molly.

"You know this woman?" Ayers asked.

Cole nodded, staring at her.

"What's her name?" the marshal asked.

"Molly Owens," Cole said.

Molly moved to the cell door and put her hands on the bars. They were cold to the touch.

Ayers said, "Keep your hands away from him, Miss Owens. No touching, or I'll have to take you out."

"All right, marshal," Molly said, stepping back. She watched the marshal leave. He walked to the end of the passageway, where he turned and looked back at her.

Cole stood. "Come to bust me out?"

"I'm looking for your son," she said.

"Buck's here?" Cole asked, coming to the bars.

Molly nodded.

"What the hell does he think he's doing?" Cole demanded.

"I think you know as well as I do," Molly said.

"Damn," Cole said. "He'll get himself killed if he tries to bust me out of this tin can."

"I know," Molly said. "That's why I need your help to stop him."

"There's nothing I can do in here," he said.

"You can get a message out," Molly said, "and I'll post it where he might see it. You can tell him to go back to Denver, or at least wait until your trial comes up."

Cole looked at her skeptically.

"I'm worried that Buck will team up with Matt Bledsoe," Molly said, "and the two of them will come in here shooting."

"You can stop worrying about that," Cole said. "Matt's shooting days are over."

"What?" Molly asked.

"Matt's dead," Cole said.

"The newspapers reported that he escaped with most of the bank money—over thirty-seven thousand dollars."

"That's the story Parlow put out," Cole said. "Down here, folks believe every word he says."

"Not everyone," Molly said. She thought quickly. "Cole, tell me exactly what happened after the bank robbery."

The pain of remembering deepened lines at the corners of his eyes. When he spoke, his words came slowly, in a low voice.

"Everything was going according to plan," he said. "We rode out of Santos to a spring south of town, where we had fresh horses waiting. When we got there, Parlow cut loose on us from a hill across the way. Pony went down first, and as I turned my horse, I saw Matt spill out of the saddle with a piece of his head blown off.

"I figured it was all over when I looked over my shoulder and saw Parlow stand up from behind a rock and draw a bead on me. His rifle must have misfired or been empty, because the shot never came. I rode out of his line of fire, right into the posse coming from town."

"Ayers brought you in?" Molly asked.

Cole nodded. "Probably saved my life, too. Now I know what Parlow's plan was. He trailed us down here and figured out what we were up to when we staked the extra horses by the spring. Then all he had to do was wait."

Cole looked at Molly. "I didn't put all this together until Parlow came up with that cock-and-bull story about Matt riding off with the loot. Now I can see that he just had time to hide Matt's body, along with the loot, and run off one of the horses to make it look like Matt got away." He paused.

"There isn't much honor among thieves, Molly, but I tell you, I never met one as low-down as Will Parlow. He's a coldhearted murderer if there ever was one, and he's supposed to be the law. Hell, he's worse than most of the lawbreakers I've run into."

"Where is this spring?" Molly asked.

Cole shrugged, then took a longer look at her. "What've you got in mind?"

"If I can find the spring," she said, "I might find Matt's body—and the money from the bank."

"Don't count on that," Cole said. "Parlow's had plenty of time to cover his tracks."

"It's worth a try," Molly said.

"What about Buck?" Cole asked.

"Ayers will spread the word," Molly said, "and most of Santos will be watching for a red-headed boy of fourteen." She added, "It'll help if I have a message from his father to post around town."

"I'll think on it," Cole said.

"All right," Molly said. "Now, tell me how to get to the spring where you were ambushed."

"Pony's the one who found it and had horses waiting for us," Cole said. "That's why he was leading the way. I'm not sure if I could ride to it, much less tell you how to get there."

"Tell me as much as you can," Molly said. "I can get help in finding the place if you'll point me in the right direction by telling me how you rode out of Santos and where you headed from there."

Molly did not say so, but her greatest concern now was not in locating the spring. She worried that Parlow would find Buck before she did.

CHAPTER XXV

Molly left a message at El Castillo's desk for Esteban. Minutes after she returned to her room, he was there at her door, asking what he could do for the señorita.

Molly repeated Cole's description of the spring in the hills south of town. "Do you know the place?"

Esteban nodded slowly. "Sí, I know of such hidden springs."

"But this one in particular is the one I want to find," Molly said. "I've been told it is about five miles south and perhaps east of Santos. It is where the bank robbers were shot."

Esteban's eyes widened. "Parlow," he said in a low voice. He went on, "I know of this place."

"Will you take me there?" she asked.

Esteban no longer smiled.

"I'll tell the hotel manager that I want your services as a sightseeing guide," Molly said. "I'll pay you."

Esteban shrugged. "The *dinero* is of no importance." He gazed at her, then said, "Sí, I will take you there."

Molly gave him two twenty-dollar gold pieces, and he agreed with a nod of his head to bring two saddle horses to the hotel. After he was gone, Molly changed into her riding clothes and strapped on her shoulder holster under her light waist-length jacket. She had bought a new Colt Lightning-model .38, and after checking the cylinder, she thrust the revolver into the holster.

Esteban was a good horseman, Molly found as she

rode behind him through the hills south of Santos. He led the way through the piñons and brush down one hill and up the next, and he sat straight and proud in the saddle, looking intently ahead.

At the crest of a hill slightly higher than the others, Esteban reined up. Molly reached the top and drew up beside him. In the narrow draw below was a dead horse. Beyond the carcass, in lush grass, was a sky-reflecting pool of water. Much of the grass had been matted down by the horses and men trampling it.

"There," Esteban said, pointing to the hilltop across the way. "Parlow was there, and when the outlaws came down this hill, he shot them." He looked at Molly. "Now you have seen this place of death."

Suddenly Molly understood Esteban's change of attitude toward her that she had seen back at the hotel when she asked him to bring her here. He thought she was morbidly curious to see the blood-stained place where the famous Cole Estes gang had been destroyed. She was a gawker, and Esteban was disappointed in her.

"Thank you," she said, wishing she could tell him the truth. "I can find my own way back to Santos."

"You will stay here?" he asked in surprise.

Molly nodded.

"I do not understand," he said. "Why?"

"It's not a matter I can discuss, Esteban," she replied. She saw his expression harden the moment before he turned his horse and rode away.

Molly watched him go, then descended the slope to the spring. She dismounted and tied her horse to a scrubby piñon nearby.

She began her search in the grass at water's edge, then moved up the hillside toward the spot Cole had described to her. Just over the top was where Parlow had concealed himself behind a rock, waiting in ambush that day.

Molly knelt and examined the dry ground. Others had been here. The soil was scratched and scraped with bootprints. She could not determine the exact place where Parlow had lain.

She stood and walked down the hill away from the spring and up the slope of the next hill. Here, in softer ground, she saw the hoofprints of a horse and a row of bootprints with them. A man had led a horse in this direction.

Molly walked down the hill and followed the tracks in the bottom of the draw for fifty yards. The tracks disappeared in the brush ahead. As she came closer, she saw that the brush had been cut and placed there.

She kicked it aside and found a small pile of stones partly covering freshly turned soil.

"Matt Bledsoe!" Marshal Ayers said. "Are you sure?"

Molly nodded, remembering vividly the gray face in the grave.

Ayers stared at her while this soaked in. "You're telling me Matt Bledsoe is buried out there?"

"That's right," Molly said. "I'll take you to the grave myself."

"Now, hold on," Ayers said. "If this is true, then you must have known Bledsoe. What's your connection with the Cole Estes gang?"

"I told you I carried a message to Cole Estes from his son," she said. "That's why I know Matt Bledsoe by sight."

Ayers gave her a skeptical look. "I've got a strong feeling there's a whole lot more to this than what you've told me."

"I haven't withheld anything of importance," Molly said.

"You weren't aware of the gang's plan to rob the bank here in Santos?" he asked.

"No, of course not," Molly said, annoyed.

Ayers studied her. "Well, show me the grave, Miss Owens." He stood and clapped his hat on his head.

Five miles south of town, Molly led the way past

the spring to the draw where she'd found the dried brush concealing the grave.

"Down there," she said, pointing to the brush. Before leaving, she had pulled it over the face of the corpse exposed by her digging.

Molly rode down into the draw and dismounted. Ayers followed. He moved up behind her and watched as she pulled the brush away. Molly immediately saw that all the stones had been pushed aside.

"Well?" Ayers asked.

For a long moment Molly stared at the loose soil, unable to reply. The grave was empty.

"The corpse walk out?" Ayers asked.

Molly turned to face him, her face warming with anger. "Marshal, the body of Matt Bledsoe was here two hours ago. That's a fact, whether you choose to believe it or not." She jabbed her index finger toward the ground. "You can see someone dug out a shallow grave."

"I see some digging," Ayers allowed.

Molly strode past him, studying the dry ground for tracks. She quickly searched the slopes on either side of the draw and then walked fifty yards down and came back. Any tracks that were here had been skillfully obliterated.

Ayers had mounted and was clearly growing impatient. "Miss Owens, I'd like to believe you. I surely would. In my opinion, you're reliable. But thinking it and proving your theory are two different matters."

"It's no theory, marshal," Molly snapped.

"I meant your theory about Will Parlow," he said. "If he killed Bledsoe, then he's the man who came out here and moved the body."

Molly exhaled. "You're right. I'm sorry." She looked around. "Without a body, there's no proof of a crime, is there?"

She went to her horse and swung up into the saddle. As they rode out of the draw to the hilltop, Molly turned and looked in all directions. The hilly landscape was perfectly suited to following someone at a distance. Now she knew that she and Esteban had been followed out here by Parlow.

In town, Molly made a concerted search for Buck. The boy might be sleeping outdoors, but he had to eat in town. Surely he had been seen here, and the sight of a lanky, red-headed fourteen-year-old would be memorable in Santos.

But after asking in every café she could find in town, Molly came up empty-handed. She felt a growing sense of uneasiness. Either Buck had left Santos, or something had happened to him. The thought that Parlow had found him gave her no comfort. The man was capable of using violence on the boy to find out who he was and why he was here.

Weary and discouraged, late that afternoon Molly walked across the plaza toward El Castillo Hotel. Across the way, standing alone, she saw a boy with his back to her, wearing a colorful serape and holding a sombrero in one hand. His hair was dark, but something about the way he stood with squared shoulders caught Molly's eye.

She made her way through the Mexican children playing on the walk that crossed the plaza and moved up behind the boy. She watched him until she was certain. Then she reached out and touched his hair. Her fingertips came away black.

"So that's how you disappeared," Molly said as Buck whirled around to face her. "Boot polish in your hair."

CHAPTER XXVI

Molly took Buck to her room in the hotel. He went with her quietly, as though under arrest. She had seen a wild look in his eyes in the plaza, as though he would turn and run. But when she spoke to him, a look of resignation came into his face.

"Just can't get away from me, can you?" Molly had asked.

Now in her room she ordered Buck to take off his clothes. From the odor that came with him, he'd obviously been living in that serape and his rumpled shirt and trousers.

"No need to be shy," Molly said when Buck cast an alarmed look at her. "I had a brother about your age, and I practically raised him."

Buck's face colored. "I'm not your brother."

"You've got a point there," Molly said. She went to the door and opened it. "I'll wait in the hall. Pass your clothes out to me—all of them—and I'll have them washed. In the meantime, I'll get hot water sent in, and you can soak in a tub." She added, "I'm curious to find out if your hair will ever be red again."

Buck cast a sheepish smile at her as she stepped out of the room and pulled the door shut.

His hair did come clean after several washings and a change of tub water. Esteban himself carried out the brackish water and brought in buckets of steaming water. Every time he passed by Molly in the hall, he looked at her with renewed curiosity.

Molly left the hotel and found the owner of a dry-goods store on the plaza who was willing to open his doors after closing hours. She bought a change of underwear, new trousers, and a white shirt for Buck. By the time she returned to her room, the boy was toweled off and ready for clothes. After he dressed, Molly took him into El Castillo's restaurant and bought him a steak.

Buck wolfed down the meal, smiling at Molly between bites. He ate an extra serving of buttered muffins, the baked potato from Molly's plate, and two portions of *flan*. Then he leaned back in his chair, sleepy-eyed.

"What was your plan, Buck?" Molly asked.

He gazed at her. "What do you mean?"

"How did you plan to break Cole Estes out of jail?" Molly asked.

Buck's eyes widened. "How did you know . . . ?" His voice trailed off. "Parlow ambushed my father and tried to kill him, just like he gunned down those men at the Outlaw Ranch."

"You're right," Molly said. "What did you plan to do about it?"

Buck paused before answering. "I figured I could bust him out myself, but I had an idea Matt Bledsoe would come back here and we could work together. I've been watching for him, day and night."

"Bledsoe isn't coming back," Molly said. "Ever."

"He ran off with the money, didn't he?" Buck said grimly. "He's probably on his way to South America right now."

"He's dead," Molly said.

Buck leaned forward in his chair. "Dead?"

"I discovered his body near the spring where Parlow ambushed those men," Molly said.

"I never heard about him getting killed," Buck said.

"No one has," Molly said, "because the body disappeared. The only reason I was able to find it was that Cole gave me an idea about where to look."

"You've seen him!" Buck exclaimed.

Molly nodded.

"I want to see him," Buck said. "I want to talk to him! Is he all right?"

"Yes, he's all right," Molly said. She added, "He's a little worried that you might do something foolish, though."

Buck could not meet Molly's gaze, and bowed his head. "I've got a right to help my father."

"Your father," Molly said, "has a way of looking out for himself."

Without looking up, Buck muttered, "I want to see him. The deputy won't let anybody in—"

"I'll talk to Marshal Ayers," Molly said, "and try to arrange a visit for you."

Buck shot a glance at her, his eyes suddenly bright with hope.

"But I can't make any promises, Buck," she said.

They left the restaurant and went to the hotel desk, where Molly paid for a second room. She handed the key to Buck. "You can sleep on a real bed tonight," she said.

Buck grinned. "Thanks, Molly."

She walked with him down the long hall and stood outside her door while Buck found his room at the far end. He unlocked the door and waved at her as he stepped inside.

Molly waved back and unlocked her door. She entered and lit an oil lamp on the wall and pulled the door shut. She jumped when a man spoke.

"Drop that handbag and turn around—slow."

Molly recognized the voice. She let her handbag fall to the Indian rug on the floor. Turning, she saw Will Parlow lying on her bed, aiming his Peacemaker at her.

"You're not the only one who can pick a lock," he said. "Now, take off your clothes, every damned stitch, so I can see how many sneak guns you're carrying."

"Get out of my room, Parlow," Molly said.

He laughed harshly. "You do play it tough, lady. I'll give you credit for that."

"You're a man who doesn't need credit, aren't you?" she said.

"What the hell are you talking about?" he asked.

"Money, Parlow," she said. "I'm talking about the money you stole from Matt Bledsoe and Pony Diehl. It must have been a king's ransom. They were carrying the Santos State Bank money and most of the Union Pacific loot. How much did it all add up to?"

"God damn you," Parlow growled. "Who do you think you are? You've caused nothing but trouble for me. Don't think I don't know about that deposition you left with the Johnson County court. You ruined me with the U.P."

His voice deepened with anger. "Damned right, I've got a pile of money in gold and greenbacks. If I hadn't stopped those outlaws, that money would have gone straight to Mexico. I've been a lawman for more than twenty years, risking my hide for the almighty *citizenry*, and what have I got to show for it? Nothing but a horse and a change of clothes and scars from gunshot wounds and knife slashes. That's right, Operative Molly Owens, I'm going into retirement south of the border, and I'm going to live the life I've earned. I'm taking the retirement that no town or county or state would give me."

"How does that make you different from the outlaws you pursued all those years?" Molly asked.

Parlow abruptly swung his legs over the bed and sat up. He took deliberate aim at her. "The talking is over. Now, strip."

"You won't fire that big gun in here," Molly said. "Everyone in the hotel will hear it."

Parlow grinned. "You'd be surprised how many people dive under their pillows when they hear a gunshot. I'll be gone before the desk clerk gets up the nerve to come down here."

Molly stared at him as he cocked the hammer.

"You'd damn well better show me some action— now!"

Molly saw his scowl become a grin as she began unbuttoning her dress front. She unhooked the neck, then the top button, and worked her way down between her breasts to her waist.

"Take off every damned stitch," Parlow said. "I want to see nothing but sweet, creamy skin."

Molly took off her high button shoes and stepped out of her dress and petticoat.

"By damn, I knew it!" Parlow exclaimed when he saw the derringer strapped to her leg. "Hand it over!"

Holding her dress and petticoat over one arm, Molly stooped down and unhooked the strap circling her leg. She straightened up and held out the holstered derringer. As Parlow reached for it, she let it fall to the floor.

Parlow instinctively bent down to pick it up, and a moment came when his eyes were off her and the revolver was aimed downward. Seeing the opportunity, Molly flung her dress and petticoat over his head and drove her knee into him.

Parlow bellowed with more anger than pain and came charging off the bed, trying to pull the dress away from his head. Molly sidestepped, stooped down, and plowed her fist into his solar plexus. As he doubled over, the revolver fired, sending a round into the floor.

Her nostrils filled with powder smoke as she raised her arm overhead and brought the side of her hand down in a slashing blow that struck the back of his neck. Parlow went down with a moan, sprawling across the Indian rug. Molly kicked the revolver away from his limp hand.

Planting her knee in the small of his back, Molly grasped his wrist, gave it a hard twist, and shoved his hand up between his shoulder blades. Parlow cried out.

Voices came from the hallway. Someone knocked on a nearby door. In a hoarse voice, Parlow tried to call out for help.

Molly realized he could probably talk his way out of this situation. She was half-nude. Parlow could claim she had enticed him into her room and tried to rob him.

Molly pushed his wrist farther up his back. "One word out of you," she whispered, "and you'll have a dislocated shoulder to show for it."

The next knock came on her door. "Somebody shot in there? You all right?"

"Yes, I'm all right," Molly replied loudly. "What's happening? I'm frightened."

"Don't worry, lady, everything's being taken care of. Just stay in your room."

The men out there moved down the hall, and she heard them knock on the door of the next room. After the voices were farther away, Molly released Parlow's wrist and swiftly moved across the room to his revolver on the floor. She scooped it up and then picked up her holstered derringer.

Backing away, Molly watched as he tried to stand. He could not straighten up. He glared at her, wincing. Parlow was in pain, but only his pride had suffered injury.

"I've never come up against a bitch like you before," he said through clenched teeth.

"Call me that again," Molly said, "and you'll find yourself back on the floor, hurting worse than you are now."

She swung open the cylinder of his revolver and punched out the bullets, letting them fall to the floor, where they rolled in five different directions. She tossed the big gun on the bed and drew her derringer.

"Where did you hide the body of Matt Bledsoe?" she asked.

Parlow stared at her, hunched over in pain, but said nothing.

"And where's the bank loot?" Molly asked. "Is it buried with—?"

Suddenly, loud pounding on the door interrupted her.

"Miss Owens! Open up!"

The voice belonged to Marshal Ayers.

CHAPTER XXVII

"Just a minute!" Molly kept her derringer trained on Will Parlow while she stepped into her dress and hastily buttoned the front with her free hand. Then she backed to the door and opened it.

Ayers came in, hand on his gun butt and a quizzical expression on his face. He looked from Molly to the hunched figure of Parlow, at the Peacemaker on the bed, and back at Molly.

"I was walking through the plaza on my way home when someone came running out of the hotel and told me there'd been a shooting." Ayers paused. "I had a feeling you'd be mixed up in it."

He turned to the open door and told the hotel men and a few onlookers from the bar that he needed no more help with his investigation and to shut the door.

"Now," he said, turning around, "just what the hell is going on here?"

"When you knocked," Molly said, "Mr. Parlow was getting ready to tell me where he buried the body of Matt Bledsoe and what he did with the money from the Santos State Bank and Union Pacific robberies."

Parlow swore and moved a step closer, straightening up now. "Ayers, I want this bitch locked up. She assaulted me."

"I defended myself," Molly said.

Marshal Ayers raised his hand in a gesture meant to bring silence. "Name-calling isn't going to help matters, Will. As a former lawman, I'm sure you understand that I'm within my legal rights to jail both of you for twenty-four hours while I complete my investigation, don't you?"

Parlow's face darkened. "As a peace officer who was running down thieves and killers when you were in short pants, I'm telling you to lock this woman up. I'm lodging a complaint against her for publicly accusing me of murder and theft—"

"Tell me, Will," Ayers said, "how did you gain entrance to Miss Owens' room? Were you invited?"

Parlow glared at him.

Moving to the door, Ayers pulled it open. "You can leave while I interview Miss Owens. Come by my office in the morning, and we'll discuss the complaint you want to file."

Parlow went to the bed and snatched up his gun. He strode out of the room, red-faced with rage.

Marshal Ayers closed the door. "I'm not sure what you got yourself involved in here, but I've got a feeling you're lucky to be alive."

"I came into my room after dinner," she said, "and found him stretched out on my bed, aiming that small cannon of his at me."

"What happened?" Ayers asked.

Molly shrugged. "One thing led to another, and I managed to take it away from him."

"Maybe I'd better change my story," Ayers said, mildly amused. "Parlow's the lucky one."

Molly smiled. "I'm glad you came when you did. He wasn't going to tell me anything, and I wasn't sure what to do with him." She added, "But I was right. He has that money, marshal."

Ayers regarded her. "Maybe he does."

Molly said, "Let's work together to prove it."

"What's in it for you?" Ayers asked.

"The court might look more kindly on Cole Estes," she said, "if the money is returned to the Santos State Bank and the Union Pacific."

Ayers shook his head. "I doubt that. He's wanted in just about every state from here to Montana. After we're through with him, there'll be a line of attorneys-general wanting to take him home with them."

"What if Cole agreed to become a law-abiding citizen of New Mexico?" Molly asked. "The governor could grant a pardon."

"Those are two real big what-ifs," Ayers said. "What makes you think Cole Estes will go straight?"

"I think he's been ready to change his life for quite a while," Molly said, "but he's never been able to see a way to do it. Cole isn't a typical hardcase, marshal. He has native intelligence, and probably could have been successful in any profession he chose."

Ayers paused. "You like the man, don't you?"

"I like him," Molly said, "and I like his son. If there was a way of bringing them together, I'd do it." She smiled. "That brings me to a request I have."

Ayers grinned. "What?"

"Buck wants to visit his father," Molly said.

Ayers shook his head, but listened noncommittally while Molly made her case. She concluded by suggesting that Cole did not want his son to do anything foolish or dangerous, and would try to dissuade Buck from attempting a jailbreak.

Ayers took a deep breath and exhaled before replying. "Tell you what," he said, "I'll let the boy in for a fifteen-minute visit if you'll give me your solemn promise to haul him back to Denver on tomorrow's stage."

Molly thought about it, and nodded. "All right, I'll agree to that."

"But will the boy?" Ayers asked with a cocked eyebrow.

"I'll do my best to convince him," Molly said. "And if my guess is right, Cole will try to convince Buck to go back to Denver too."

Ayers nodded and moved to the door. "Bring the kid at ten A.M." He pulled the door open and said over his shoulder, "And tell that boy not to try anything dumb. I'll personally search him before he goes into my jail."

In the morning, Buck was at first excited by the

news that he would be allowed to visit his father, but then he protested strongly when Molly explained the condition. Not until he had realized that there was no alternative did he agree to it.

"It isn't fair," Buck said in a low voice, "but I'll go along."

Molly heard a distinct lack of sincerity in his voice.

Marshal Ayers had not been joking when he said he would search Buck. Upon arriving in the marshal's office, Molly was invited to leave them alone.

"You'll have to shuck those duds," she heard Ayers say to Buck as she stepped out of the office.

A few minutes later the door opened. Marshal Ayers came out, followed by Buck. The boy's face was still red from the embarrassment of a strip-search. Molly watched them cross the room and climb the stairs to the cellblock.

The clock on the far wall ticked off exactly seventeen minutes; then the barred door at the head of the staircase opened. Buck came down. Ayers locked the door and jogged down the stairs behind Buck.

At the bottom, Buck whirled to face the marshal. "You can't make me leave town! I haven't done anything wrong!"

Molly hastily crossed the room and put her hand on Buck's shoulder.

Buck went on, his jaw jutting toward the marshal. "I have a right to stay for my father's trial!"

Ayers glanced at Molly.

"He's right," she said softly.

"Yeah, I reckon he is," Ayers conceded. "But I won't allow any more visits. The next time you see your father will be in a courtroom." The marshal strode past them and went into his office.

"What did Cole tell you?" Molly asked.

Buck bowed his head. "He doesn't want me to stay. He says it's all over with him, and I ought to go back to Denver and finish my schooling." He looked at Molly, his lip quivering with emotion. "I can't leave, Molly, not now."

"You don't have to," Molly said. She put her arm around his shoulders, and they walked to the big double doors of the jailhouse. As they approached, one of them swung open.

Molly blinked, momentarily blinded by the harsh glare of morning sunlight. A shadowy figure was there, a tall man wearing a low-crowned hat.

"You stinking bastard!" Buck exclaimed. "I'm going to kill you if it's the last thing I ever do."

"It will be," the man replied casually. He stood there in the rectangle of bright light, a looming, menacing figure. "Next time you see me, either wear a gun or turn tail and run."

The man stepped inside and brushed past them. Molly had recognized his voice, and now she glimpsed the profile of Will Parlow's weathered face.